THE FORBIDDEN DREAMS OF BETSY ELLIOTT

THE FORBIDDEN DREAMS OF BETSY ELLIOTT

A NOVEL

Carolyn R. Parsons

FLANKER PRESS LIMITED
ST. JOHN'S

Library and Archives Canada Cataloguing in Publication

Title: The forbidden dreams of Betsy Elliott : a novel / Carolyn R. Parsons.
Names: Parsons, Carolyn R., author.
Identifiers: Canadiana (print) 2018906739X | Canadiana (ebook) 20189067403 | ISBN 9781771177252
    (softcover) | ISBN 9781771177269 (EPUB)
Classification: LCC PS8631.A783 F67 2019 | DDC C813/.6—dc23

PRINTED IN CANADA

MIX
Paper from responsible sources
FSC
www.fsc.org
FSC® C016245

This paper has been certified to meet the environmental and social standards of the Forest Stewardship Council® (FSC®) and comes from responsibly managed forests, and verified recycled sources.

Cover design by Graham Blair

FLANKER PRESS LTD.
PO BOX 2522, STATION C
ST. JOHN'S, NL
CANADA

TELEPHONE: (709) 739-4477 FAX: (709) 739-4420 TOLL-FREE: 1-866-739-4420
WWW.FLANKERPRESS.COM

9 8 7 6 5 4 3 2 1

Canada

Canada Council for the Arts   Conseil des Arts du Canada

Newfoundland Labrador

We acknowledge the [financial] support of the Government of Canada. *Nous reconnaissons l'appui [financier] du gouvernement du Canada.* We acknowledge the support of the Canada Council for the Arts, which last year invested $153 million to bring the arts to Canadians throughout the country. *Nous remercions le Conseil des arts du Canada de son soutien. L'an dernier, le Conseil a investi 153 millions de dollars pour mettre de l'art dans la vie des Canadiennes et des Canadiens de tout le pays.* We acknowledge the financial support of the Government of Newfoundland and Labrador, Department of Tourism, Culture and Recreation for our publishing activities.

For Dante, Dominic, and Aleena:
You are the magic.

ONE

Though a speck against the backdrop of the earth, her body framed by the broad, biting Atlantic Ocean to the west and a battered shoreline to the east, if the sky had eyes and could see all things, it would have paid particular notice to the young woman on that cold Monday in November.

She'd marked time like a soldier, spending her days taking all the steps asked of her without ever advancing. Oh, the same could be said of most of the people who lived in her island community on Newfoundland's northern edge, but she differed in that she harboured no delusions about it. Had she been a man, she would have become a soldier, thinking it preferable to die in battle than live with the constant sameness that permeated her life. But it was what it was. She'd march in place and die here, and that was that. So, she carried on, ever moving, going nowhere.

A southwesterly wind blew across the ocean, its bite leaving a tattoo of pink across her cheek. She stopped twice to pull her headscarf forward, but it slipped off each time, and she gave up. Rounding the bend into the second cove, the wind now at her back, she marched forward on the loose beach rocks, pails clink-clanking against the water hoop. The circular metal band, taken from a large barrel, kept the buckets steady and prevented them from knocking against her legs.

The woman hated this part of her trek. The stones were too big and rounded for easy walking. She wished she could throw them into the ocean and bare the smooth bedrock beneath. It was a short beach. She could hunker down and just heave them, whoosh, plop, ripple, over and over, until a smooth surface remained to make the walk easier. Oh, the ocean would toss new stones onto the beach, smoothed and presented like gifts to the shoreline, but it would take many years. She sighed. As usual, she didn't have time to do anything she wanted to do, so it was no good to think about it. She knew the route by heart, and though the hated stones rolled under her feet, she never stumbled. Each step forward was a victory.

Her mother always said there was something wrong with folks who lived in their head with thoughts of things they couldn't do or see. *You got to face life as it comes, because you don't get to go nowhere. Do the work put before you, keep alive, and don't think things can be different than they is. Now, you can make some stuff go your way when the time comes, but you're never going to be able to walk too far from here, so you might as well keep your head here, too.*

But the girl never paid much attention to all that. She could stop her mind from thinking what it thought no more than she could stop the tide from heaving the broken glass from sunken ships ashore. The beach glittered with bright green and blue pieces of bottles between the rocks. Tiny treasures that came only because nothing could stop them.

* * * * *

A few yards ahead, the young man determined that the sky held a threat of rain, but he figured it might hold off for a while. He was sheltered from the wind in a cubby between two rocks, pencil scratching on paper, risking a wetting to get something down. Clouds gathered overhead, stacked like the quilts his aunt had banked upon him that night last week when the temperature plummeted and she feared he would freeze.

A moment later, a young woman carrying buckets scratching against a hoop was upon him. Jarred from his deep concentration, the man found himself caught in the glare of flashing black eyes. A bit of water splashed from the left bucket, but she regained control of it and herself in one motion.

"You needn't scare me to death." Her dialect made the word *death* sound like *det*.

"Sorry, I thought I was all alone here in the morning," he replied.

His accent was like when you took syrup and added water, the woman thought. Not as sweet, yet somehow tasting better than before. It was soft—almost British, almost Newfoundland.

"No trouble, then." She nodded and moved to carry on.

The man sat back against the stone and watched her strong back, his eyes flicking up to her shoulders. There were no houses for quite a distance. Surely she wasn't going all the way to the Elliotts'?

"Hey!" he shouted. "You need a bit of help?" He jumped up and jammed his paper and pencil into an inside pocket, stumbling and slipping in his effort to catch up with her.

With a near-imperceptible shake of her head, she replied, "No."

Committed now, the young man brought himself up alongside her. "Where are you headed?"

There it was again, that soft accent, part Newfoundland and part somewhere else. The somewhere else intrigued her.

"Where are you from?"

"Here," the man said. "Well, used to be. I've been away for years. Boston, and most recently St. John's, but Boston is home."

"I knew you was a stranger. Never seen anybody here wearing anything like that." She nodded toward his fine grey overcoat.

"I got it in New York. Oh, that sounds pompous, doesn't it?"

"A bit stuck-up, yeah, but I loves cities," the girl said, her sigh diminishing her usual sarcasm. "I haven't been to one, but I reads all I can, stories about all those people and shops and cars. Must be some nice."

"It *is* nice," the newcomer replied. "But it can become tiresome after a while. It's nicer here in many ways."

"Who's your people?"

He stumbled on a rock and righted himself. The girl stopped, too, her shoulders tightening from the weight of the buckets.

"The Hoffes. Garland and Geraldine. Garland was my father's brother."

"You're a Hoffe?"

"I use the name Taylor now. Edmund Hoffe Taylor. Mother thought it best I line up with her family when I was trying to get into Harvard, so she changed it."

The young woman lowered the buckets, then straightened up again before setting out.

"Hey, you should let me carry that for you."

"Sure, I can carry this. I does it all the time."

"Well, I can do it for you, give you a break. You're a girl."

"I'm twenty-two!"

Edmund glanced at her slim figure, unable to see the lean muscle of her arms and shoulders under her coat and the strong calves snug against her boots from the girth of her legs, where days of physical labour had built them like a man's. A pretty face from Boston appeared in his mind for a moment, and he stumbled again. The girl before him pretended not to notice, but a grin tugged at her pursed lips.

"Yes, but I'm a *man*," Edmund said. Men in his circles always cared for the ladies around them. His sense of chivalry insisted that he carry this load for her. Plus, it would be easier for him. He was stronger.

Her eyes looked ahead to the flat of the stone that lay ahead, aware that around this bend was the worst part of the walk. The wind would be in her face the entire way. She considered the wisdom of allowing him to carry the pails. He wasn't used to it. She needed the water and didn't fancy going back to refill her buckets should he trip and spill them. But that smug face of his tempted her to let him try. Perhaps he could do it, though he looked as soft as a down pillow with his fancy suit, pretty lips, and that silk hanky peeking out of his coat pocket. But she might never get another offer again in all her life. Grab what's before you, as her mother always said.

"Yelp." She stopped.

"What?"

Edmund turned to her. It took a second to realize that she had said yes. He was still unused to the thick Dorset he had not heard nor spoken since his teen years. She was already setting down the pails and stepping out of the hoop.

"Well, go on then," she encouraged, admiring the square of fabric poking out of his pocket. She had never touched silk before and wondered what it felt like.

"All right." Edmund took her place between the pails and reached down for the handles.

"Oh, ouch," she said.

"What's wrong? Are you hurt?"

"Oh, I've just some dirt and a splinter in my hand. I'll pull it out when I gets home." She held up her hand. "If I had something to wrap it in—"

Edmund pulled the handkerchief out of his pocket and handed it to her. "Please, use this."

"Oh my goodness, thank you." The young woman accepted it, wondering at the ease with which she had appropriated it from its owner. It had E. H. T. stitched on it in fancy letters. She recognized the lettering from a book on penmanship she had at home and from which she had spent hours practising. She could embroider a similar thing into something for John for Christmas, perhaps. What a fancy thing it was.

She rubbed the buttery smoothness between her fingers, enjoying the softness, then hurried after Edmund, who was stumbling ahead with her buckets. He hoisted himself upon the smooth rock that stretched for about fifty feet before it got rough again. She grinned, remembering how her legs had groaned and hurt for days the first time after that step up.

Gulls swooped and shrieked overhead, and the clouds attended to business elsewhere, leaving a matte blue sky behind. The young woman quickened her step to catch up, fingers still stroking the silk in her hand, but duty motivated her to be close to catch the water should he stumble. Also, the pebbled beach up ahead was the most difficult to walk on with the buckets. He'd soon give up and ask her to take over.

Or fall arse over teakettle trying, she thought, her grin breaking into a full-fledged smile.

TWO

Sensing Edmund's discomfort with her trailing so close behind, and not wanting to heighten the risk of his stumbling with the water, she skipped forward on the tree side of the shore, where the mossy ground was soft and damp. The sun had yet to dry the dew off the short juniper bush that reached and spread its claws out to scratch anyone who got too close. Her step was sure on the loose grey rocks; her heavy-laced boots took care of that. Edmund's fancy city shoes weren't doing so well. He was slipping and trying to keep balance on the rocks beneath his feet. He'd made it over Flattie—her nickname for the smooth rock path—but now he had Elliott's Beach to cross.

She paused a few yards ahead of him and peered over the water, shading her eyes with a hand. A ship was making its way westward. Its stacks—two of them—traced against a backdrop of sky and distant land. Farther down the run, a large schooner made its way in the opposite direction. Its sails fanned out, hiding the blush of the horizon. She figured it was a Twillingate boat sailing home after being hauled ashore for repairs and painting in what was commonly called being "hove down."

Yes, it looked bright and freshly painted. It was too late for fishing, and too early for the seals that came in droves to these shores in early spring with the northern ice floes. The number of schooners and steam vessels in the Wester' Run had dwindled as fall faded. Ships were fewer these years as people abandoned them for land prospects. Some people around the islands speculated whether the place would survive another twenty years. So many were leaving it all behind and moving away for *opportunity*, a word half the town said with awe and the other half with derision.

She looked back at Edmund. His steps were purposeful as he balanced the pails of water. She looked again at his shoes. Most people wore boots. Shoes were for soup suppers and church on Sunday, with only the wealthier, fancier, older men donning shoes at other times— like for meetings and such. None had any like those Edmund sported. They were shiny, black, and peeked out from under his tailored pant leg. Old Mrs. Elliott had described Mr. Coaker to her once, telling her about the time he had come for the first annual meeting of the Fishermen's Protective Union in '09 and how fancy his suit and shoes had been. Perhaps these were the same sort.

Edmund, too busy focusing on each footstep to notice her intrigue over his shoes, glanced up to find her staring at him.

"What? Disappointed I haven't tumbled over yet?" He smiled to hide his fatigue.

"No, you haven't . . . yet." The young woman's eyes met his, and he saw that grin for the first time.

"How far is it?" Edmund figured it must be around that bend ahead, in the next cove.

"Oh, we goes around two more coves, through the meadow path, around the hill, and down the garden. Nice piece, yet. Want me to take the buckets back now?" she asked, noting the look of dread on

Edmund's face. "But you're a strong man. You can do it for sure, if I can. 'Tis a hard path, but not that hard."

"Oh yes, I can do it," Edmund replied. It was a challenging trail, and he wondered how long he could handle the stretching pain in his shoulder and the aching fatigue of his legs and back. Perhaps an even graver concern, if the meadow was soft and wet, what sort of damage would it do to his shoes? The path widened enough to walk side by side, so the girl stayed next to him.

"Tell me about Boston."

"What in particular would you like to know?"

"How big is it? What is there to do? Do you go to movies?"

"I don't know the exact population right now. It's a big city. Up until I left, I attended the university, so much of my life was at the college. I do go to movies, and I have a lot of friends. We visit each other's houses and play cards, or music, and have dances. The houses are big, and some have a room for dancing. But there are smaller houses, tenements, and even slums. The men go to hockey games a lot, and I met Eddie Shore once after a game. Nice fellow."

"You met him? The hockey player?"

They could only get hockey news from the paper. There was nothing much on the radio station; their cove received a signal marred by static. Not that it mattered. She'd heard the station would soon be bankrupt like the rest of St. John's. Her household cheered for the Toronto Maple Leafs and hated the Montreal Canadiens. But they liked Boston's Eddie Shore, and if they weren't for Toronto they would be for Boston. All this and they had never seen a single game played, only the odd bit of commentary and scores recorded in the papers they received when ships could get in with the news.

Edmund, surprised that this girl knew who Eddie Shore was, prepared to regale her with stories of his own prowess on the ice. But his breath caught in his throat, and he realized he was working too hard at carrying the water to talk so much.

"Yes," he murmured in response to her question. He stepped with care, shifting the weight of the pails on his shoulders. The buckets were heavier with each passing second. Wondering if he should stop for a spell, he considered that if he did, starting again might be more difficult than continuing. He'd said he would carry the water, and by damn, he *must* be as strong as this pretty girl.

He straightened his back and made his way up the rocks to the flatter part of the beach. There the moss melded into grass with a well-worn path. This appeared to be an easier section. Once up there, though, he was open to the wind, and it took him in the face. He struggled to keep his balance.

"What's your name, anyway? Excuse me for not asking before, miss."

"Oh, I'm an Elliott." The name rolled out like a song. It was hers, and how she loved it. "Betsy," she added. She had practised her new last name many times since before this land was hers. Betsy loved her maiden name, Crane, too, but only for her late father's sake.

"Elliott," she repeated, her voice proud.

Edmund didn't know of this Elliott girl and hadn't known the Elliott son—what was his name? John, yes. *Guess he married.* This daughter would have been born before he left home, he figured. Odd he hadn't known.

"You have sisters and brothers?"

"Had." The wind whipped at her face. Its cold fingers traced the tracks where tears had once fallen for her siblings but were now dry. Betsy looked at the ship again as it steamed along far out from the shore. "Come on, b'y," she shouted, the steel back in her voice.

Edmund didn't ask more. Children died easily, but most families were large enough that some remained. He sensed that in Betsy's family this wasn't so.

"Coming along." Two words were the most he could manage as he tramped across the meadow. His hat, though tugged by the gusts, remained on his head. His shoes imprinted the soft path as he put his feet one after the other. He was careful, not because of the uneven ground, but because he wasn't sure he could trust his legs to hold him up.

Betsy's grin returned when she saw how tired he was. There were two more coves to go, and then the hill path, which was narrow, through the long garden. She trailed along, her hand clutching her scarf as her hair blew up and around it. She took in the tall grasses, the wind-caught branches rustling, the absence of clouds in the north sky, and the starkness of November, even on a day as fine as this one.

Edmund's arms screamed for rest, his shoulders burned, and his feet ached. His shoes scraped against his heels, galling them. But he carried forward, blisters, stubbornness, and masculine pride as his companions.

Betsy walked just far enough ahead to hear his laboured breathing, the occasional grunt, and the deliberate step of each foot as though it were his last. Head down, she moved sure-footed through the coves and around the hill until they entered the garden path that was the last leg of the journey. The house loomed ahead, and when she turned toward it, following the crook in the trail, she spotted John working near the schooner. The boat would soon head down to the tickle to be secured for the winter. The seas were too rough to fish with December almost upon their shores. John walked up the path from the wharf. He headed to the house and reached it before they did.

Betsy led Edmund toward the steps and grinned at John. "Edmund Hoffe Taylor," she said, pointing to her helper.

John Elliott reached out to relieve the young man of his buckets.

Edmund straightened his hat and pulled his jacket back into place. His fine, light grey pants were muddied halfway up to his knees, and dirt dulled the shine of his patent-leather shoes. There was nothing he could do about that.

John handled the buckets as though they were filled with feathers. He lodged them up on the long bridge that wound around the house. Edmund groaned, relieved.

"Sir, it's a pleasure to meet you." Edmund held out his hand to John Elliott, then winced at his grip.

"Sorry," said John, who turned his hand over and sucked in a breath at the red galls from the bucket handles on Edmund's palm. "Well, 'tis work you're not used to, b'y. I heard you were from the States."

"Yes, I admit 'tis not an easy job." He smiled at Betsy, jubilant because he knew she expected his failure. She would look lovely in a Boston dress, he thought.

"Well now, you go along with Betsy. She'll fix that right up. She's a good one with the salves for sure. Makes them herself." His voice held significant pride in Betsy's medical prowess.

Betsy led Edmund into the house and motioned for him to sit at the table. He pulled a hard wooden chair out and eased his sore body into it.

"Here is the salve."

Betsy put it on the table, then realized that she should administer it. She pulled out the opposing chair and sat. Taking his hands and tipping them palm up, she reached into the little jar with two fingers and pulled out creamy ointment. Taking her time with each hand, she rubbed some on, soothing their blisters. She pulled a rag bandage out of a drawer in a cabinet and wrapped both palms. Ripping the fabric down the centre lengthwise, she tied it around his wrist to secure the bandages.

"Don't do much with those hands until they're better," she cautioned as she gathered her things and started back to the door. "I got to get me wash done and out on the line, and it's almost eight already. Sure, Phoebe White will have hers out first and they'll all think I'm dead. Why don't you go see Skipper outside for a chat? He'll be some excited about that hockey. Loves to talk about news and stuff and will be right interested in you."

"Would he?" Edmund rose, testing his muscles to do just as she had commanded. But her next words had him sitting right back down again.

"Oh, sure," Betsy said, heading off to a room behind the kitchen. "My husband loves stuff like that."

THREE

Husband? Surely John Elliott was old enough to be her father. The hard chair pressed into the strained muscles of his back, and his hands throbbed under the bandages. Edmund clenched his fingers into a claw, then straightened them. There would be no typing for a few days. No writing of any kind.

Muffled women's voices chattered over the swishing of water against a scrubbing board in a room beyond the kitchen. Edmund could distinguish Betsy's, though he couldn't decipher the words. Her voice, husky and deep, issued directions. A resolute silence followed the end of her sentences. He pictured her back there, sleeves rolled up, strong arms moving up and down against the scrub board.

A young girl of fifteen or sixteen stepped into the kitchen. She pulled on some knitted slippers that rested near the stove, then lifted the lid to stoke the flames within.

"Betsy says I have to wake the boys now." Her soft voice sounded strained, like she hadn't used it in a long time.

"Oh." Edmund swallowed and cleared his throat. "The boys?" He wasn't over the shock of Betsy being married to John Elliott, and now to learn there were children!

"Oh yes, sir, two little boys, and the youngest needs feedin', and

Betsy's aching for him." She placed the poker on a hook behind the stove and moved toward the bedroom. The outer door opened, and John entered. Wizened and grey-haired, Edmund guessed his age to be around fifty.

Edmund stood up but then sat down again when his back spasmed. John grinned at him. "Jaysus, b'y. Not used to it, is you?" His smile knocked a decade off his features. He was a good-looking man, all told, and despite the age gap, Edmund could see how a young Betsy wound up marrying him.

"No. I haven't hauled water since I was a boy and never walked that far with it." There was something contagious about the island accent, and his own became more prominent while chatting with this man in his kitchen. The dropped R's of his Boston dialect became foreign and unnatural as he yarned with John, though he'd spoken that way for most of his life. His vowels broadened, but his H's had a mind of their own, plopping down wherever they felt the need to be and yet non-existent in places where he had for years articulated them well.

"Lugging those buckets would probably kill me," John said. "Betsy's strong like an ox."

"Yes," Edmund agreed.

John Elliott also moved like a young man. He was strong from hard work. His body had not an ounce of spare flesh. He settled on the daybed in the kitchen, already with a day's work done, to rest for the next part.

Edmund got up again. He flinched at the soreness but stood all the way. He inquired after his missing shoes.

"Oh, the women likely took 'em to spiff 'em back up."

"Should I go and get them?"

"They'll bring 'em by an' by," John said.

"Perhaps I should. I should be getting along and let you have your nap."

"Nah, b'y, nar nap now, just a bit of a laze. You sit back down. Your people are the Hoffes? Your mother from Boston?" He knew the answers, but it was polite to ask.

Obeying, Edmund sat and answered. "Yes, Father was a Hoffe. Mother was a Taylor. Boston Taylor, but her family was from here to start. I go by Taylor back in the States."

"I remembers your father. Yes indeed, a fine man. Yes sir, he was. Gone a long time now. You both moved to Boston? You and your mother? After he passed on?"

"Yes. Mother wanted to go home to her family when he died, and they wanted her back. I have been in St. John's, though, for several years now. Got tangled up with the politics there. Interesting times, b'y," Edmund said with a shake of his head and a grin.

"Oh?" John sat up.

"The place is in an uproar about the commission and all that."

The province struggled under the financial difficulties wrought by staggering debt, so the decision had been made by those in power to forfeit responsible government and return to British rule under a commission. It was a blow to those who valued Newfoundland's independence and held a belief in democracy. Though this wouldn't be official until the new year, the votes had been cast and the decision was final.

"Did you go down to the Colonial Building? Did you march on Duckworth? Or is you a Squires man?"

"Can't say I'm anybody's man, but I did go down. Never saw a crowd so wild."

Betsy swept into the kitchen, two little boys toddling behind her. She sent them off into the next room by tossing a small wooden bobber in for them to play with. She pulled out a pot and set it on the stove. Her skirt moved around her in an unchoreographed dance as she called for Mary to come get the boys so she could cook dinner.

"You'll be stayin," she said in the general direction of Edmund, who nodded, though an affirmation wasn't needed. Her words were a command.

". . . the weasel was lucky. Crooked as he is, 'twas a wonder he wasn't murdered." John had carried on talking, and Edmund pulled his attention back to him. He loved how John pronounced *crooked*. He loved this dialect. It was curious and quirky. It was home.

"'Twas the constabulary, you know. All was quiet until they started batting the sticks around, beating people off the steps, and things exploded. It was bloody mayhem after that."

John was sitting up straight. He brushed a hand through his full head of silver- streaked hair, his eyes sharp and piercing. "Tell me. We are stuck out here on this rock, only gets a bit of radio we can't hear for static, the papers come when they can get here, and people talks, but what's going on? How bad is it?"

The pot hit the stove with a clang. Edmund jumped, and both men looked to Betsy.

"Betsy, come and listen," John said by way of invitation, knowing full well she demanded to be part of the conversation.

"I can hear you," Betsy said, satisfied.

"Good, maid, good." John nodded for Edmund to carry on.

"Well, it's hard to know. But it's bad and getting worse. The merchants won't starve, I suppose, and the rich don't care much, anyway. But for the people, the regular people, there are no jobs, no money for them. Squires was right on one thing: the country can't go on like this. Some says we should go back under England, and others thinks we needs to have a say and that England will starve us more if we go back. There is talk of war again, too. Some days I think you can't give up nationhood forever, and 'tis beyond consideration not to have a vote."

"'Tis desperate, is it?"

"Yes, 'tis desperate, and it's worse outside the city. I was visiting Mr. Albert's—you know them, they're Mother's people—they're starving and, well, with the new development—" His face reddened as he trailed off. Mr. Albert Sharpe, crippled from rickets he contracted when he was a boy, now expected baby number ten. That was the "development" Edmund couldn't bring up in front of the missus. That visit haunted him. He had never been in a house as cold or as sparse, or with children so thin and sickly. And his poor wife looked worn out. The Elliotts' large, warm kitchen with its oversized stove and pretty curtains in the windows was a mansion alongside Albert Sharpe's place.

"Betsy brings the babies in with the midwife, Old Julie. No need to be shy about stuff around her."

"Oh, I see." Edmund squirmed, still embarrassed, then continued. "Sir, it's desperate in Newfoundland. There is more like Mr. Albert than there is like my Uncle Garland, and it will get worse."

"What did you see at the riot last year? Did you see Squires?" The former prime minister had been embroiled in scandal, accused of stealing money and falsifying cabinet minutes, and the protest took place in April of the previous year.

"I was at a meeting the night before the riots broke out. It was a planned march, just a parade, and I was there as an observer. I wrote everything down, as I felt it was history, and I wanted my own record beyond what was in the *Telegram*. The papers were all on the side of government. They must own them, if we know the truth of it." That was a common refrain now. Edmund had no evidence that the local newspaper was leaning toward a certain side in the whole mess, but he suspected it was so.

Betsy checked the pot, replaced the lid, and returned to where the men sat.

"Tell us," she said, her voice steady.

"Okay, well, he said it was a clarion call to arms, Mr. Howell did. He said we were in ruin, or would be, and saving the country was up to the brotherhood—and sisterhood—of Newfoundland."

He looked at Betsy, who nodded.

"I have it written down. The speech." Edmund pulled papers out, slipping a sheet free. He handed it to John, who passed it to Betsy.

"She's a better reader," he explained, though it was his eyesight more than his level of literacy that made her better.

Betsy read, giving no heed to the men, knowing they would listen. Her voice was strong and clear as she read Mr. Howell's speech.

"The force operating in our midst today, if allowed to continue, will surely bring the country amongst the breakers. Whilst the sails may be in ribbons, the heart of the ship is sound and can be saved. But wiser and more sincere men than those in power are required to bring her back on the course of her destination. As at the feast of Belshazzar, the handwriting of doom is on the wall, and it comes to us today with disturbing frequency. It could be seen on the walls of the banking houses, the businesses, and the factories."

Silence.

"Lot of big words, but I knows what he means," Betsy said after a moment. "That's in the Bible. They could have been saved, but nobody knew what the writings was. Kind of means there has been clues all along, but nobody could tell or would tell. Fancy speech, but true enough."

"Yes, that's what it means. How did you know?" Edmund's surprise at Betsy's comprehension showed on his face.

She handed his papers back. "What? You think we don't know anything? One thing we knows is our Bible, Mr. Boston Harvard man!" She strode over to the stove, lifted a lid, stirred the contents, and slammed the cover back on the pot.

"Betsy knows everything that can be figured out from any books, and plenty more, besides. We got a good many books here in this house. Mother was a big reader." John grinned at poor Edmund. The young fellow was in a heap of trouble for underestimating his Betsy.

Mortified, Edmund stammered, "I'm sorry, I didn't mean . . ."

"Howell is right," John continued. "I sees it right here on this island. People who always had enough can't make do no more. Them that had more than enough is not so well off, and we're in that crowd. Then the crooked Squires made more than the island's total wages for a month's work, paying himself in tax dollars, when the dole isn't enough to feed the starving. Politicians that could fix it is ignoring it all. 'Tis like this in every cove around the island. The hard workers needs the dole now instead of just the sick. Oh, I sees it all the way here, and I would have marched that day, too. But the ones who could make it better ignored it far too long."

"Is that what your book is about?" Betsy asked Edmund.

"Yes. I recorded it all. A lot didn't make the papers. People were beat up and hurt. I have their stories to write down. And I have to do some papers for the university to finish up things there. I want to do it, and maybe one day they'll print it for the people to see. Unfortunately, I'm leaving again as soon as I can get a run back to Lewisporte. I intended to stay the winter, but it's not worked out."

"Oh? What happened?" John asked.

"I came home because I have so much to write, and I thought I would do it here, where it's quiet. But with all the youngsters, turns out there is only a daybed in the room behind the kitchen at Uncle Gar's, and while they're good as gold, there is no quiet place to write. I told them I'm leaving, and they understood. He's got boys enough to help him out, and they're in a good way compared to some."

"You can do it here. Work on the paper for school and your book, too," John said. Betsy gave him a look.

"Our old bedroom is shut down. We haven't a use for it. We took the big room when Mother died. It's quiet, and there's a little writing table. It's in the attic. The bed is good, and there is a washstand. A bit colder than our room now on the eastern side of the house, but still not bad."

Betsy moved to the pot on the stove and hauled off the lid. The nerve of John making such an offer without talking to her first! A boarder. For the entire winter! The steam dampened her face, and she pulled back. The heat only added to that which brought her blood to a full boil.

She pulled the plates out and set about her work putting tea on the table, then called for young Mary as the men carried on with their talk. John would feel the lash of her tongue on his hide later when that Edmund fellow left, that was for sure.

Betsy heard the name Cashin bandied about as a hero as she set salt cod and fried potatoes on a plate. Hero? For telling the truth? She wanted to say something. Tell them what she thought of that union man, Coaker, and the local man, John Henry Scammell, who both aligned with that no-good Squires. Crooks, the lot of them. She knew, though, that if she started, she would wind up telling them both what she thought of the government and John's invitation to the young man from Boston. With some difficulty, she kept her mouth shut while she took up some food for herself and joined the men at the table. Betsy's temper stayed up until John said the grace, at which point she stifled it for later.

After John had returned from his evening's work and was reading the paper in the parlour, she spoke loudly to the serving girl, Mary.

"We're likely to have Mr. Edmund Taylor as a boarder this winter for the writing of his book and papers. You're not to tend on him at all. He is a soft city boy who has to learn to pull his weight. Also, don't shine his shoes anymore. He can do it hisself. Oh, and Mary, we will need you in the winter after all, on Mondays and p'raps more."

Mary nodded, both happy and terrified. What would she ever say to a fancy Boston man? She had scarcely been able to eat while he was at the table, so nervous was she that she would do something wrong. But her crowd sure needed the money, and he was nice to look at, with his perfect smile and nice eyes.

Betsy worked her way around the kitchen. She was glad Mary could stay. It eased her on Mondays to get out of the house and get water or do outside stuff she couldn't do with two small youngsters. But she didn't fancy a strange man under her roof who expected to live like he was still in Boston. For sure in Boston he was tended to all the time. As if she didn't have enough work to do without another man.

She jammed a junk of wood into the stove, sending flankers into the air. She swatted at them like they were annoying mosquitoes and slammed the lid back down. Feeling contrary at this turn of events, she determined she'd keep every damned cent of his board for herself, too, since she was doing the work, and she'd tell John that the first minute she got him alone. If she saved up, she could buy a nice piece of cloth down at Earle's and make herself a brand new dress for Easter. Yes, that's what she would do. Or perhaps order a store-bought one from the catalogue, though she thought in her own mind that those she made herself were nicer than anything sold in the Army and Navy. She'd get a hat, too. She was only slightly less angry when she joined John later that night to prepare for bed.

FOUR

"Are ye cracked?" Betsy snapped at John later that evening.

John was lying atop the covers with his clothes still on. "Oh yes, missus, cracked broad open." He slapped her rear end as she walked by.

"Stop it," she commanded. "What were you thinking, askin' the Boston boy to stay here for all the winter? He's another mouth to feed. We couldn't keep as much grub as usual. The price of fish was that low, we didn't stock in near as much. But you knows all this. Can you never say no to anybody?"

"Missus, there was no *no* to be said. I offered. I could use the help. He needs a place. He wants to write his book and study, too. Harvard, Betsy. He's right interesting to talk to, you got to agree with that. Nobody from this place went to a fancy school. He is funny, too, said that Mrs. Squires was the best *man* amongst 'em in the riot." He grinned as he recalled the joke.

"Well, I dare say she was, but that don't change nothing. I don't understand you, John, inviting a stranger into the house. Sure, his crowd might be right fronted by that." In a small town, Betsy knew it might insult his family for Edmund to leave his own people's place for theirs. It might start talk that would look bad on the Hoffe family.

24

She'd have to visit them and make sure there were no hard feelings. *Oh my, so much trouble.*

"The Hoffes is good people. They knows what's right. They won't care, and he's writing important stuff. The country is falling apart, missus. We needs hands here for the work, and one more won't hurt. And he'll pay. There'll be money for Mary, and they needs it for sure, and you can have her regular again."

"We needs hands in summer, not now. And work? The boy couldn't lug the buckets. He's nish."

"Hardly nish, Betsy. He's the opposite of that. Sure, he lugged them buckets with galls on his hands and feet when most would have cried."

"Well, I can lug it easier."

"You're used to it, Betsy maid. You're stronger than most men."

"Why do we need him at all, then? I can help with the work." She had softened with the compliment.

"What if I gets sick? You and the youngsters all alone? Look what happened to Martha Hart. I hear she's puttin' young Samuel on the boat for the orphanage when it goes, so she can go into service. Afraid he'll starve here with Simon gone and no people to help her out. I'm older, Betsy. Another body in the house is a good thing."

John looked at Betsy from his perch on the bed. On her young face, lines of strain had set around her mouth like crevices in stone. He waited as she calmed. She hung her clothes on a hook and, with her back to him, washed her face and underarms and breasts. John felt the stirring in himself that her lithe movements created. He knew he needed to let her calm down before acting upon it or she would shut him out for the night, and he wanted her too much to risk it.

"Betsy, maid, I thinks it's the right thing. But if you wants, I'll tell him no, that I changed my mind. But if you lets him stay, I'll make sure he pulls his weight around here. I'll have young Mary get the room clean, keep her an extra hour or two. I'm sure her crowd could use any extra coppers. We have enough in until April, and he'll go away again when the ice is off. Perhaps this year I'll take a berth on a sealer. If I gets sick, I'll be better again by then."

Betsy fingered the soft flannel gown, thinking. She hesitated, but her body yearned for touch, and her anger lessened. They hadn't starved yet, though when he got sick she always feared he'd stay that way. She lowered her nightwear and turned around to face him.

"No, you can't go back on it now. I don't like it much, but we'll deal all the same. I'll talk to young Mary and set it all up. Give me a couple days to get things straightened and get that desk down for him. 'Tis a nice desk, good to have it out, but it might need some fixing. It had a loose leg when we put it up there."

"I'll get that down for you tomorrow. You come to bed for a bit of a cuddle."

"A cuddle? I don't know you'll be gettin' nar cuddle from me, John Elliott," Betsy said, but his nice smile and dark blue eyes had her thinking she might want a bit of a cuddle herself.

John sighed when she didn't put her nightdress on. She walked over to the bed, dropped the gown at the bottom of it. Wearing only her bloomers, she climbed under the quilts. He turned to her, tickling her to make her laugh, kissing her. When the mirth died, she stroked his back as he reached past her and blew out the lamp. And then her anger was all but forgotten as he stroked her thighs, the round of her buttocks, the curve of her shoulders, and then moved himself atop her.

Some time later, Betsy located her nightgown and slipped it over her head. John climbed out the other side and walked to the basin and washed himself with the tepid water, then hauled on the bottom of his two-piece underwear. He padded back to the bed, shivering, his steps like a toddler's, and climbed in beside Betsy. He cozied up to her back, and she didn't throw him off, allowing him his cuddle. She would move away from him before long, but his embrace warmed her, and she relaxed into it. John's snoring filled the room within minutes. Betsy counted down from ninety-nine, a trick she used to put herself to sleep, and was soon breathing deeply of the cool air, her mind quiet for the first time in seventeen hours.

FIVE

The wind shifted and blew in a straight line down toward the tickle and the road through to Elliott's Cove. Edmund sported a fine tweed winter coat, double-breasted, and cinched at the waist with a wide belt. On his head sat a warm fox fur hat that came down past his brow, and around his neck was a store-bought scarf tied to the left. His thick, rich leather boots had an intricate scrolling design on the outer sides. He carried a case in each hand as he strolled up the path to the Elliotts' home.

"Fancy," Betsy said after a sidelong glance when he entered.

Edmund ignored her sarcasm and pulled off his boots. He was growing accustomed to her disapproval, and it didn't bother him as much once he realized she pretty much disapproved of everything.

"I'll clear up the floor," he said in response to a scowl at the mud that flicked off his boots.

"I would," she replied.

He stood and started to clean up with a mop perched in the corner by the door. When he finished, he looked around the large kitchen of the house that would be his home for the next couple of months.

Betsy eyed the large square case next to his suitcase when he wasn't looking, wondering if his typewriter was inside, a machine she'd never seen before. She would check that out later.

She returned to her sewing machine, which was visible through the door opening into the parlour. She positioned some fabric under the needle and started the machine going. John's mother had taught her how to operate it as a young girl. She had been kinder to Betsy than Betsy's own mother had been. Betsy had been eager to learn about this magical black machine with its gold scrolling design and the word SINGER emblazoned across the top. She fancied it was called a singer because the rhythm her foot made on the large pedal was a song to her. Sewing was a pleasure, not a chore, she loved it so. Eventually she was gifted the machine.

"Betsy, my love, you used that machine better than I ever could. It'll keep you in pretty clothes, and you deserve it," the kindly Mrs. Elliott had told the orphaned young girl. Betsy was already being courted by John, and the old lady wasn't sure she approved of the match, for Betsy's sake. But the girl was like a daughter already, and if she married John, he'd be taken care of. She didn't say so back then, but the old woman thought it might prove to be a way to earn her keep should John not be able to provide for her at some point, given his health and age. Betsy's talent far surpassed any other women on the island, and so Mrs. Elliott told the ever-grateful Betsy, whose eyes stung with unshed tears at the best present she'd ever received.

Now, years later, nimble fingers pushed the fabric along without thought. A low fire burned in the parlour stove, but she sat far from it. The sewing heated, satisfied, and calmed her.

The whir of the machine created a metronome of up-and-down clicks as Betsy's leg worked the pedal. Edmund watched her skirt rise and fall, rise and fall, up and down, and was mesmerized by the motion. He jumped when the door opened behind him.

"Ah," John said, "I feared you wouldn't have good winter clothes. Nice and warm, they looks." John didn't notice the coat's impeccable style. "Betsy is sewing over some of Father's old clothes for you. You can't be working in those nice shirts from Boston, and there's a lot of work to get at. Ever mend a net, b'y?"

"Long time ago, but I'll get it back."

"Well, we got days of it, and I got no sons to give me a hand. Well, none big enough yet. A man can't be sitting at a desk all day. You'll seize up like a dried sculpin." John had Edmund's winter planned. He could write for a few hours in the morning, using daylight to save oil and candles. But then he'd go into the store loft to mend the trap, help with the wood, and perhaps tend to the horse. John had a bugger of a time harnessing the contrary old mare. Edmund could yank the belts tighter and keep her steady for him while they rigged her up.

"Give our boys a few years." Betsy looked up from her machine. "They're smarter than most."

"Yes, clever boys, but not big enough to do the nets yet, and I hopes they never got to. Perhaps they'll get schooling and leave here," John agreed, his smile fading at the thought.

"I hope so," Betsy said.

"I see no reason two smart young boys couldn't do well in a Boston school, or in St. John's," Edmund said.

"Oh, you don't, do you? What about the fact that they got to go to Labrador with their father when they're—what, ten or eleven? If they survives that and don't get the idea in their head that fish is all there is in the world, because that's all there is in the world we lives in, well, then there's the money needed for 'em to go. I'll see they gets all the schoolin' they needs to go off, if they chooses, but hardly no one ever goes from here."

"Well now, Betsy, young Art Scammell is going to make a go of it. There's some."

"Yes, John, *some*. I hopes they makes it, but odds is against it, you know. There are lots of things to fool up a boy's chances of ever getting away into the world, and even more if we ever has a girl. She's got no chance at all."

"What about Ida Parsons? She's gone off."

"A rare woman, she is. Not many so smart as Ida Parsons."

"You is, Betsy. You're as smart as anybody I ever met."

"And I'm stuck here listening to your old foolishness, now, aren't I?"

"Yes, and I got more old foolishness for you later on." He winked. "But first I have to make a needle for the Harvard man, Betsy."

"Oh?" Edmund drew a chair over from the table to sit and watch what he was up to.

John pulled a rectangular piece of wood from the pocket of his jacket hanging on a peg by the door. "Here, b'y, hang your coat on that one." He motioned to the other peg that sat between Betsy's coat and his. Edmund stood, hung his hat and his jacket between the two shabby coats, feeling an inexplicable pang at the difference between his and theirs. His eyes darted to Betsy, who was busy at her machine.

"I have extras, but they're worn out, b'y, plus a fellar should have his own." John sat and pulled the small knife from his pants pocket and opened it. He slid it along the side of the wood to test it, shook his head, and pulled a small square stone from beside the chair.

Spitting on the dense grey stone, he rubbed the blade over the spit, wetting it, then started filing his knife with quick, deft movements.

"God's truth is I'm not sure if I can still make a needle outta wood anymore." John's eyes twinkled, and he dabbed his calloused, dirt-grained thumb on the edge of the knife, nodded at its sharpness and set to work.

He sized up the wood as though gauging where the needle might be. Betsy watched as he shaved the excess off. He was a master wood-carver. The boys had an assortment of boats and animals he'd made from bits of wood when the time allowed on cold winter days. Edmund noted that John hadn't sketched lines on the wood as a guide. Starting in the centre, he just carved. The veins in his aging hands filled with blood as his nimble fingers chipped and cut away anything that didn't look like a netting needle.

Edmund let out a breath after he finished. "I thought for sure you were gonna split it there when you were cutting out the prong part."

"The hardest part, and I've split the wood before." But not since he was a boy. He'd never had a thought it would break.

With the needle complete, the outside edge carved and smoothened to perfection, John carved E. H. T. on it at the bottom, near the shallow "U" shape, handed it to Edmund, and winked.

"There you are." He grinned.

"Thanks a lot, John. That's wonderful. Now I just need a net to work on."

"Now you needs clothes," Betsy stated. She handed him pants and shirt, hemmed and mended.

"Thank you." Edmund looked at the netting needle and the pants. "Fine job, both of you."

In a household where thank you didn't pass between people much and where doing for each other was a necessity, John and Betsy were unsure how to respond. Betsy headed to the kitchen, and John stood and stretched before heading to the back window facing the bay. Edmund rose, picked up his belongings, and walked toward the stairs.

"Come out in the store loft when you're straightened away, Edmund, b'y," John said by way of invitation as he walked toward the door. "I got the fire goin', and there's work to be done."

Nodding, Edmund headed upstairs. He entered the bedroom where he would spend the winter writing and changed into his new clothes. It had worried him that he only had his fine shirts and pants. Despite this kind gesture, he pondered on Betsy and her obvious discomfort with his presence. Perhaps in time he would win her over. He sorted his clothes into a low bureau, then hung a suit in the wardrobe. He placed his shaving items on a washstand that held a basin and jug patterned with tiny yellow roses. A soft towel hung over the rack, and a bar of soap sat to the side.

Finally, Edmund hoisted the heavy case upon the bed and opened it. He lifted out his prize possession and set it upon the desk before placing several spare ribbons in a small drawer. He arranged the rest of his writing supplies and stacked paper beside the typewriter, then sat for a moment, testing the chair and adjusting a small flat cushion. Inserting a sheet of paper into the machine, he poised his fingers on the keys. Then he pulled back, moved the chair away, and stood, deciding he would start writing tomorrow morning. Right now he needed to get to the store loft to help John.

"You're going over already?" Betsy was kneading bread.

"Yes. I thought the writing could start in the morning."

"Good idea. See you at dinnertime."

Edmund replied with his own farewell and left the house, heading toward the store, feeling pleased that he had finally done something of which Betsy seemed to approve.

SIX

Several weeks later, Edmund had settled in. The sun broke through, and he looked down from the second-storey window. The little alder that grew just below sparkled with a hoarfrost that draped over it, decorating it in a Christmas shroud. Edmund pulled the blanket he had wrapped around his shoulders closer, working up the nerve to remove it. He should have banked the fireplace the night before, but as usual, he had fallen into the bed, exhausted after a day in the woods with John. He'd shivered through the morning's writing as the meagre heat from his lantern barely kept his fingers from freezing in the cold room. It lit the room in the cloudy pre-dawn.

The papers on his desk were a formidable stack, his solid three hours every morning paying off. Guilt rushed through him at the sound of hustling outside his door while he pecked at the typewriter. Betsy always rose before him, and the smell of her morning's cooking tempted him to cut his writing short. His stomach agreed, and he threw the colourful patchwork off and straightened it over the pillows. He'd caught Betsy making his bed one morning and couldn't bring himself to allow her to do it again.

Edmund relieved himself. God, he hated using a piss-pot—or chamber pot, as nicer folks called it. As much as he hated pissing into a bowl where a thin film of ice had caught over last night's urine, he hated a trip to the outhouse more. He missed electricity, streetcars, motor cars, and the bustle of lights and parades that filled his Boston Christmases. But he was getting his work done without interruption, and that was the most important thing.

He opened the door to the kitchen. Betsy hesitated in her work, then resumed rolling bread buns into their pans. How early had she been up to have it ready for its final rising? In houses with a big family, the women baked bread every day, but Betsy did so only on alternate days. Around the kitchen sat a variety of jam tarts. The pantry, too, had been filled with fruitcakes and pies that tempted him every moment of the day.

"Tea is steeped."

Betsy was in the habit of getting it ready for him but always refused to sit with him to drink her own. Instead, she moved from one task to another as she worked, never idle, never still unless she was rocking little Richard to sleep. This early, though, the boys still slept.

Edmund grabbed cups and set them on saucers. He used a towel to pick up the teapot, and as he poured, Betsy spoke. "Sure, if you could have waited a minute . . ."

"I s'pose I can pour the tea, now, missus." Edmund knew she hated for the men to do anything in the kitchen, but with her hands in flour, she couldn't do it herself.

He pulled out the plate from the warmer where she always left his breakfast. She made it early on when she cooked for John, and he appreciated the large amount.

The chill left Edmund's body in the heat of the kitchen, and he unbuttoned his light cardigan. He needed a homespun garnsey, the kind of warm sweater all the men around here wore, knit by the women, but everybody was so busy, even young Mary, so he hadn't bothered to ask somebody to knit him one. After Christmas, he thought, he might buy the worsted and pay her, or even Betsy, to do it, though he worried about her workload. He knew she would do it, and the money would help. Still, he hated to impose.

He ate breakfast, grateful the toast was fresh and soft, toasted by hand on one side over the open flame, the way he preferred. Betsy had predicted the time he would arrive at the table and had made his fresh, which he appreciated, though to say so would earn him a hard look. It seemed these people didn't know what to do with a *thank you*. Helping each other was a given, not a gift.

"Sit and drink your tea, Betsy."

Betsy wiped her hands in her apron and turned to him.

"Yes, perhaps I will," she replied.

Edmund's eyes widened. She'd refused his invitation every day since his arrival. "Got some sewing to do," she said. She pulled her cup of tea close, mixed dark brown sugar into it, then carried it by its saucer to the chair near the stove. In moments her quick fingers worked on a shirt that sat on a table by the fire.

Edmund pushed his chair back from the table and took his tea to join her, swallowing the last bit of toast. Her eyes met his before returning to her work.

"What are you making?"

"Shirts for the boys for Christmas."

"Is the machine broken? Want me to look at it?"

"No, I'm putting their letters on 'em, see?" Betsy held up the shirt in her hand to show where she had embroidered the boy's monogram into the collar. Then she reached to the side and pulled out another small shirt and handed it to him. The embroidery on this one was complete.

"I'll give you back the handkerchief now. See how I made the letters fancy like on that? It's like letters in a book the old people—John's parents—had. I thought p'raps it would be nice for Christmas shirts for the boys. The blue is for Richard, and green is for George."

Edmund held the blue one. He ran his fingers over the perfect tiny stitches.

"Oh, you can keep the hanky," he said, and didn't catch the sparkle of delight in Betsy's dark brown eyes. "This is wonderful work, Betsy, better than what is on the handkerchief, and so nice for Christmas."

"I made up the stitch myself. Bit different for the cotton, but the letters look good, don't they?" She was being cautious to pronounce things, substituting the *th* sound for the *d* because she knew it was the proper way. Betsy wasn't perfect, but she listened to Edmund's manner and copied it, though Edmund would often drift back to island language when he talked to John.

"It's wonderful," Edmund answered with a smile. His blue eyes met hers and held them, his admiration as obvious as the letter on the collar of the small shirt.

"Betsy, you have such a talent. Who taught you?"

"Well, I knew how to sew since I can remember. Mother was good at it, but she only liked to make old-fashioned stuff. I likes to make what I see in the catalogues. I put my own touch on them." Betsy dropped the shirt and grabbed several catalogues on a shelf next to the machine. She came back and flicked to a page marked with a small piece of yarn and turned it so Edmund could see.

"Here, I figured out how to make that. I used old pieces of flour sack and made a pattern and made different sizes of it drawed on there. I have it here." She patted a folded white bundle of fabric that was the basis of the dress she indicated. "Then I can make as many as I wants of that size. I make each one just a little bit different. Instead of the lace in the picture, I crochets my own with patterns Mother taught me and adds it to the collars. John's mother loved pretty dresses and travelled a lot when she was young. She talked about custom dresses and helped me learn. I like making dresses. I wishes I had cloth to make more, but it's pricey, and where would I wear it to, anyway? Oh, I s'pose you don't want to hear more about dresses now, Edmund." Betsy put the catalogue back, her eyes following her hands as though returning the book to the shelf was the most difficult thing she had ever done.

"I find it very interesting, Betsy. Do you draw out all your dresses? On paper, I mean."

Edmund noticed how Betsy flipped her speech to more local mannerisms when John or others were around, but when it was the two of them, she spoke more like him. *So do I, though*, he thought, knowing well his own penchant for slipping into his first dialect with John but back to his Boston tongue with those who spoke a softer dialect like Betsy. He realized she might learn from him, so he adjusted his speech on purpose so she got the Boston Edmund, not the Newfoundland Edmund.

"Oh yes, but paper is scarce, so I have to be smart about it. Here." She handed him several scribblers with drawings of dresses and ideas marked through the pages.

"I know little about ladies' fashion, Betsy, but I think I like the way you did the neckline here, and that jacket is prettier than anything I've seen in Boston. These are all from your head?"

"Yes, well, when would I see them for real? I'm sure they're not so good as what the ladies in Boston is wearing, though. You're tormenting me now." Flattered by his words, she was sure he was teasing.

"It's as good as I've ever seen. I swear to God."

Betsy's pleasure showed on her face as she put the books away. She could only dream of creating her dresses for real, but it was a good dream, and it kept her from going stark raving mad. She stayed awake at night in the long winters, imagining and drawing with great detail in her mind. If only she had more paper and fabric.

"Is Mary not here today?"

"She's needed at home this morning." If Edmund noticed she didn't pronounce it *dis marnin'* anymore, he didn't let on. "How is the writing going?" Again she spoke with just a slight accent. She leaned back as he talked of his work.

"Well, the paper for the university is done. I was smart and got that out of the way first. It was almost done, anyway. The book is coming along, too. Hardest part is taking all the research and making it fit into fewer words." He gave her a description of events that he'd condensed into interesting anecdotes.

Betsy wanted details. The one time he had tried to scoff her off and give her a revised version of what he was writing, she accused him of treating her "soft," so now he provided more information. As he talked, he looked away, his mind back in the time of which he wrote—the politics, corruption, losing a country—and he talked until her chair ceased to rock. Betsy had fallen asleep with a small fold of fabric in her hands, her breathing silent in the warm room.

Before Edmund could get up to leave, the door opened. The wind blew across the big kitchen, and John laughed as he caught it with a foot, his arms filled with wood. Edmund jumped up to help and motioned with a nod to Betsy, fast asleep. John winked and kept his steps light on the floor as he put the logs, one after another, into the box beside the stove. Edmund closed the door with a gentle pull.

John sat and hauled his boots off before the fire, pulling his socks back up as he did. Edmund made his way to the stove to pour tea into a cup and then set about clearing the dishes off the table. It was still early, but John had worked up an appetite, and with a quick glance at Betsy and a second wink at Edmund, he motioned to the pantry. Edmund topped up his cup and was ready when John returned. John placed the contraband on the table and pried open a tin can that had a picture of Queen Victoria on it. With an eye on the rocker, he added margarine and plates and encouraged Edmund to eat up.

Knowing the man of the house would take the brunt of Betsy's wrath for looting the goods she had charged them to leave alone, he sliced off a thick piece of a dark fruitcake and put it out next to the wedge of jam tart John had put on a plate for him. He smelled the sweet fresh berries picked earlier in the fall. With grins firmly in place on both men's faces, they settled in like two mischievous children and had a feast of Christmas baking, hot tea, and cold rum.

Afterwards, they put the rest away with a forced stealth hampered by the rum swishing around in their stomachs. Glancing around the kitchen, John picked up the bottle and motioned with it toward their outdoor clothing. They rushed when they heard the boys chattering in the room. Drunk on sugar and rum, the men sped toward the store loft and let loose with a roar of laughter when the door was shut behind them.

"She's gonna kill us," John said, his eyes twinkling as he took the lid off the rum lid and swigged at it.

"She's gonna kill *you*," Edmund corrected.

"Betsy's not sweet like the other missus was, for sure." John poked at the fire still burning in the drum stove from the morning.

"The other?"

"Oh, I had a Labrador missus one time. Got sick and died. Not strong, like Betsy. She was same age as me. I learned you gotta have a young hardy wife, b'y." Betsy always grumbled to him that he couldn't say no to anybody, and one of the big regrets of his life was leaving his first wife in Labrador at summer's end for several years because he couldn't refuse his father, an overbearing man whom he had spent all his life obeying. "Lost me youngsters, too. But now I have two more," John added, his mind far away in Labrador, in a time gone by.

Edmund drank more rum and changed the subject.

"She's gonna kill you for this."

"Nah, b'y." John was glad to return from his reverie.

"Oh yes, stone dead. Or you'll wish you was."

John thought for a minute. "I knows what Betsy needs!" he declared.

"You do?"

"Yes, b'y, come on."

"What? Let's sit and finish the rum." Edmund was enjoying the warm glow flowing through his bloodstream as much as the warm heat from the oil-drum stove.

"Bring the rum. We have to do something so Betsy won't kill me." John said it with such seriousness that Edmund felt he must surely take part in whatever life-saving plot John had in mind. He hauled his coat on again and fastened it, slapping his hat on as John did the same.

John tripped on the ladder and caught himself with the hand that held the rum. Edmund staggered along behind him, ready for their excursion.

Snow lay in clean banks over the land. They followed the path and passed the rum back and forth, weaving along, drunk but with purpose. It was a good thirty minutes later before Edmund knew what the plan was, and he agreed it was the best thing to do for Betsy—and to stop her from killing John, stone dead.

SEVEN

The bright blue sky cheered the morning, and John and Edmund couldn't help but be in a jovial mood as they walked. Their breath disappeared in a puff as they headed out on John's great mission.

"They got to charge him with murder if he dies," John said, referring to a great disaster whereby Eddie Shore of the Boston Bruins had knocked Toronto Maple Leafs player Ace Bailey out in a game a week prior, nearly killing the man. It still wasn't certain he would live.

"He was after Clancy. He didn't mean to hit Bailey. 'Twas hardly murder," rebutted Edmund, an avid Bruins fan.

"Mean to or not, fellar dies, 'tis murder," John argued, not hoping the man would die, but knowing the Leafs would have a better time against the Bruins if they locked up Eddie Shore.

"I'm sure he'll live. He was quite a gentleman that time I met him, and I'd hate to see him in jail for this." Edmund also hoped he wouldn't be kicked off the team. Fighting was part of the game. Perhaps a game suspension would be fine, but a man in jail over a hockey game didn't seem fair. "That one?" He pointed.

"No, the best ones are up on the mish," John said, using the old Dorset word for marsh, which had come across the Atlantic with his ancestors.

"Well, that looks good to me." Usually Edmund deferred to the older man, but the rum had made him cocky.

"It has to be perfect." John walked fast, and Edmund struggled to keep up with the taller man. "Writing coming along?"

"Oh, yes." But Edmund's thoughts were back at the house with Betsy. John's revelation about a first wife and her subsequent death had been in his thoughts, and his rum-loosened mouth had to ask. "She's not sick, is she?"

"Who, b'y?" John was still thinking about the hockey game and Eddy Shore, and it took a minute. "Bets?"

"Yes. I never saw her fall asleep before." What if she had tuberculosis? A woman had been sent off in the fall to the sanitarium for tuberculosis patients in St. John's.

"Oh, no, not sick, b'y. Betsy's fine." Betsy hadn't had any excuse to stop his advances for a while now, so he figured she was bringing another youngster. But he didn't want to tell the young man that. "She's busy with the boys and the Christmas cookin'. Betsy's tough as nails. All her crowd is good stock."

"Who is her crowd?"

"Betsy was a Crane. When her father, Roland, died of the fever, her mother, Fanny, had to go in service. Betsy was only ten, then, grew up here with us. I come home one fall and she was a woman. Now, I never touched her until we were wed and she was eighteen."

He glanced at Edmund. John had had only one concern about having a young man in the house—that he would be after their young cousin, Mary. He didn't seem the sort to go after a young girl, but you couldn't be too careful.

"You can't be at a young girl, b'y, you know?"

"Oh my! No, sir, I never ever would."

Edmund's shock was unmistakable, and John was glad of it.

"'Tis not right. Bert Snow got a young woman, way too young, only fourteen, and she died with the birth. Too young and it kills the girl. Bets was at that birth and was right savage."

"He married a fourteen-year-old?" Edmund's face registered shock.

"Yes, b'y, and Father signed to allow it. But she was already in the family way, so had to, I suppose. Bets was some bad over that. One of her first births she tended to before we was wed, and she was ragin'. The girl should have been left alone."

"It's not considered murder, I suppose, but it should be. Did the child survive it?"

"Yes, the little girl is with relatives, though. Father wanted no part of it, and good, too. Anyway, we were talking about Betsy. She come with her mother, Fanny Crane, from over the bay. She was the oldest, and the other girls, her sisters, was sent on the boat to St. John's to the orphanage and then was took in by two different families, far as we know. Betsy won't talk of them."

"She sent her own children away? How old were they?" Edmund, taken aback by the callousness of that, wondered what sort of mother would do such a thing.

"Only small. Twins, just four. We would have took the youngsters, too, but Fanny said they would be in the way. That Fanny Crane was a hard woman. She was a good worker but mean as a snake, putting those youngsters on the ship." He thought of his own boys and took a swig of the rum to wash away the idea of it. "So, the two of 'em worked here in the house, and I was in Labrador from spring till fall, and me missus there died, leaving me with no wife."

"Then you married Betsy. You never considered marrying the mother?"

"Nah. She was old and not fit to marry. God knows poor Roland Crane had a tough time of it. Mother took Betsy on and kept her clear of Fanny, stepped between her and the belt a good few times. If it wasn't for Betsy, Mother would have sent Fanny Crane off—and meant to as soon as Betsy was old enough to take over the work. But old Fanny's heart gave out one day, and we done right. Gave her a burial and kept Betsy on. I tried to find her sisters for her, but no luck."

"That was good of you both."

"Mother was not good in health. Old man was gone. I needed a young hardy wife, b'y. I wanted sons and maids, too. Lots of 'em, if I can. I liked Betsy best, and her mother had been all for it, too, before she died. We wed when she turned eighteen, and we had George eight months later, and no, like I said, I never touched her afore. He come early."

John thought back to that first night, when Betsy had been frightened like a kitten and he had tried not to hurt her. She had laid there unmoving, letting him do what he wanted, and he had done it, unable to resist but knowing it wasn't the way. He'd watched her wash the blood from herself before they had settled in to sleep. Her hair had been past her waist, and her breasts had been firm and high. She had smiled at him and pulled a nightgown over her head. All maids hurt the first time, but John had felt like a monster. His first wife, Mere, had been a widow and had taught him how to take care of a woman. John had wondered if she liked to be touched, so he stroked her hair and had asked if he could make it feel better for her. Betsy hadn't answered, so he had stroked her breasts and then moved his hand to where she hurt. He was gentle, like Mere had shown him, and he felt her stir, enjoying what he was doing.

Edmund's voice dashed the memory away.

"That one?"

"What? Oh, no, over there." John motioned with his chin. He pulled another swig from the bottle, and this time he put the bottle in his jacket pocket.

"That one is better, John," Edmund argued. He headed across to where he had pointed.

"That's on the dam. You can't go across there, Edmund. 'Tis not sound."

"It's froze solid, b'y." Edmund, sure the ice could hold him, and happy to have in their sights a tree suitable for Betsy, dodged off toward it.

"No, that's deep and don't freeze." John's stern warning went unheeded as Edmund headed off, determined to get the tempting fir.

John felt the hit of the rum on his legs, but his senses weren't affected, and he knew there was no way the ice would hold the young man.

"No! Get back here!" John shouted, picking up speed, attempting to catch the defiant fool. He heard an unmistakable noise and stopped. With a *crack-crack-crack* sound, a fissure formed in the ice. The tracks of it spread from Edmund's boots like sunrays, creeping away from him, its epicentre. A second later, he shot straight down into the icy pond.

Enough light filtered through the hole above so he could see the mud particles and bubbles moving around in silence before him. Through the murky water he could make out the tangle of beaver sticks that formed the dam. The cold hit with a deep shock that penetrated through to the marrow of his bones. His boots filled and dragged him farther down. Panicking, he kicked, trying to knock them off. He failed, but the motion pushed his body upward. He kicked harder, the light at the top serving as a beacon while darkness closed in on his oxygen-starved brain.

Edmund's head broke into the air with a whoosh. He coughed muddy water and inhaled in large gulps. The cold sliced into him, and the rum vanished from his bloodstream. He grasped at the edge of the ice, but it crumbled in his numb hands. The weight of his boots dragged him under again. He tried to kick them off by using one to push at the other, and he bobbed to the top once more.

"Stretch your arms wide, like this," John shouted a short distance away.

"I can't," Edmund gasped, turning toward the voice. Needles of cold stabbed him so deeply, he wanted to escape into the darkness.

"Listen to me, goddammit!" John was harsh, desperate, and firm.

Edmund's panic settled at his tone. He heaved his arms open and sprawled against the ice as John indicated. By doing so, the edge of the ice could bear the weight of him better.

"Now kick your feet like you're swimming. Use your feet to push yourself up!" John was flat on his belly, stick held out, inching toward Edmund. He mimicked an awkward swimming motion, an odd lesson from a man who couldn't swim a stroke.

Edmund kicked and kicked, exhaustion and cold crawling over every inch of him. John's voice ordered, cajoled, encouraged.

"Come on, b'y, you can do it. Kick. Kick hard!"

Edmund wanted to stop trying, but John would not allow it. Every inch took a mile's energy. John also moved forward, getting as close as he could without endangering himself.

After a while, Edmund's chest found solid ice, and he rested a second. His torso followed with further effort. When he could reach the stick, John pulled it, but Edmund was too weak to hold on. He heard a crack as the ice broke again. His body numbed as the water rose over his body once more. He prepared to slip back into the icy pond, this time for good. Before he could whisper the prayer that would ensure his fast transport to the right part of the afterlife, he found himself up and out of the water, dragged by one hand, bit by bit, to the far side of the pond, sliding forward as John Elliott backed up on his belly, dragging him.

Edmund lay on his back, shivering, the taste of dirt in his mouth. John took a breath, too, winded from the effort. He looked at the waterlogged, bedraggled man and shook his head.

"Lucky the beavers didn't come and chew your feet off your legs, b'y," John joked, but his face was serious.

Edmund's blue lips split into a grin. He hoisted himself up and pulled off his boots, emptying the water from them. John helped him up once he had hauled them back on his feet.

"Got to move, b'y, you're fair bivvering." John pulled off the younger man's jacket and shirt and put his own warm coat over him. He wrung out Edmund's wet clothes and tied them in a bundle on the axe handle. The coat hung long on Edmund, which was a good thing.

He walked by himself for a while, then John helped him along. The movement increased his blood flow, but the exhaustion and cold got to him before they made it home. He collapsed in the garden.

Betsy saw them coming up the path and swung the door open.

"What is wrong with him, John? Did he fall overboard?"

"As good as," John replied.

Edmund lay on the daybed, and Betsy set to stripping off the rest of his clothes while John fetched what had dropped in the garden when he collapsed. Edmund came to but was too cold for modesty. Covered in several warm quilts, he shivered. John stoked the stove while Betsy tended to him. He hauled off his own damp garnsey and stood in front of the stove to warm.

"Should I go get Old Julie?"

"Not yet, John. Let's see what I can do for him first. Get the knitted blanket in the parlour. Is the fire up good?"

Edmund's lips were the dark purple colour of the sky just before a storm rolled in. He shivered but was conscious and would live if he didn't take a fever. Betsy rubbed his limbs, starting at the top of his legs and pulling down to bring the circulation back into them one at a time while her two little boys stared at her, already aware that when Mother worked, you stayed back.

"I'm fine," Edmund rasped. "John wanted to get you a Christmas tree."

"Where, Grassy Islands?" Betsy asked, referring to two islands just off their shore.

Edmund laughed. "Beaver Pond."

"Fir trees don't grow in the bottom of the Beaver Pond. Guess they don't teach that in Harvard. Some damn foolish to drown for a stalligan," Betsy joked, using a local word that referred to the useless scrawny fir trees that struggled to grow branches in their harsh weather. They were no good for burning nor building. She shook her head, but her humour was a good sign, John knew. The boy would be fine.

"I'll tell them to put it in a syllabus. It's something every lawyer should know," Edmund said, laughing at his misfortune.

"I think he's improving," Betsy said.

"P'raps this will help, too." John held the rum bottle out to Betsy, risking her wrath. Its contents were well down now. She had bought it for medicinal reasons, but if it could help Edmund, he'd take the risk.

"Yes, it certainly will. That's exactly what's needed," she said.

Betsy wrapped a strong hand around the neck of the bottle, put it to her lips, and drank it dry. Beside the kitchen table, two youngsters stuck their thumbs in their mouths and watched the three laughing adults.

EIGHT

Late Christmas Eve, 1933, the wind screeched lynx-like through cracks in the eaves. It rattled the door latch like a beggar trying to get in. A savage storm had whirled its way across the ocean and now battered the shores of northeast Newfoundland. The snow squalls still swirled outside Christmas morning, leaving a roil of patterns piled up against the stilts that held the house fast against the rocky hill. They laid a blanket across empty flakes—the large platforms for drying fish—like a bed prepared for some great giant.

Betsy kept her shawl around her, cinched at the front with her mother-in-law's pearl brooch. A matching comb clip held her hair in place. Betsy had claimed both, to the chagrin of John's only sister, who lived in Twillingate and couldn't get down to stake ownership of her mother's personal belongings. Everything had been left to John, Betsy explained in the letter he'd asked her to write. Betsy wore it knowing John would always stand up for her, given the care she'd given his mother and that they hadn't heard tell of his sister until there was jewellery to be distributed.

The parlour warmed up, and she kept the door between it and the kitchen wedged open with a small chair. She tucked oranges into the little socks hanging by the fireplace, then placed homemade lassie candy into each one, a treat she made only once a year by dropping molasses in snow to harden. Underneath each sock she set a small wooden boat carved by John.

Betsy ran her hand over the surface of the smooth wood. It was soft like the skin on her little sons' cheeks. She nodded at the small tree she had cut herself and fitted onto crossed sticks to keep it upright. The decorations she'd strung on included some lovely flowers cut from wallpaper remnants found in the attic.

Handmade gifts lay beside the hearth in front of a stack of wood piled high so nobody would need to bring any inside on Christmas Day. Despite the blowing snow, a smattering of sunshine lit the morning. Betsy surveyed her parlour, which was shined to perfection, and basked in it and the peace of Christmas. Four little feet padded down the hallway, and she rushed to meet George and Richard, huddling them close for just a moment. "Merry Christmas, my boys," she whispered so as not to wake the men, but her stealth was for naught. John followed close behind, sniffing the air, the smell of food tempting him out of bed on this rare opportunity to sleep late.

"Smells some good, missus." He scooped up a boy in each arm. Their giggles caused Betsy to shush them and laugh at the same time.

Edmund strolled out and seconded the older man's sentiment. "Merry Christmas!" He inhaled the aroma as well. His eyes twinkled, blue and merry. He looked citified in his crisp white shirt and good pants. It was Boston Christmas attire, Betsy supposed.

He smiled with his perfect white teeth, something she marvelled over. Her teeth were still good, but she was young and might have trouble before she was his age, like most of the folks in town. John's were going, though he still had his front teeth, and they were straight for a man of fifty.

Edmund caught Betsy staring, but she didn't look away, and he dropped his eyes. His windburned face matured him and gave him a more rugged appearance. An unfamiliar sensation in her belly made her as blustery as last night's wind had been. She shooed them all into the parlour and headed for the kitchen, whipping on an apron over her nice dress to finish up the big breakfast she'd started.

John and Edmund each laid small gifts near those she had left. Edmund had enclosed his in coloured paper with each of their names on them. He also had brightly coloured packages for the boys.

"Kettle's on the stove, grub is under control," John hollered. "I don't think these boys can wait another minute for their presents. Sit down, Betsy, and let's see what Santy Claus brought!"

"Oh my, I suppose. Give me their socks. Come on, George and Richard, let's see what you have."

"The pretty ones, Mother!" George said, eyeing the merrily wrapped presents left by Edmund.

"Oh, open the stockings first. Go on," Edmund said, fearing the parents would be insulted if his gifts were opened first.

"No, open those first," Betsy replied, as excited about the pretty packages as were the boys. John was already handing one to George while Richard looked on, happy but confused, not realizing what it was all about at just two years old.

"Don't tear the pretty paper, George. Help Richard, Edmund, but don't tear it. It's pretty. I can save it for something else."

"All right, Betsy. Come here, Richard." Edmund held out his arms, and the boy, already fond of their kind visitor, lunged into them, curious about this thing he held.

"Wow, Edmund boy, you sure went all out for the boys." John was on the floor with George, examining the tiny train that the child held. It had an engine and several cars.

"Richard's is different. I had them sent out from St. John's. Got somebody to put them on the real train, then they came on Earle's boat. You can get more cars to attach to the back, see, to make it go. And if you press the button, it makes a sound."

John pushed it, and George jumped when a loud *woot* came from the tiny engine. Then he pushed it himself.

"Well, that's the best thing I seen in a long time, Edmund. That was some good of you."

"They're good boys, and I thought they might have fun with trains. I like them myself."

"I do, too. I was only on one the time I had to go to St. John's to the Waterford Hospital for—"

"Come on, let's open the rest," Betsy cut in.

"Yes, let's open them all," Edmund said. He was curious why a man like John would have been in the mental hospital. Surely he hadn't had problems like that. No, he must have been visiting somebody.

"Betsy and John, this is the nicest garnsey I ever saw," Edmund exclaimed a few moments later, after opening a sweater from the Elliotts.

"Betsy done all that. I only knits vamps," John joked, knowing Edmund would know he didn't knit woollen socks.

"That's some nice needlework, missus," John said after opening his new shirt with an embroidered monogram on the collar just like she'd made for the boys.

"You'll all look some nice in church tonight," Betsy said, watching the boys.

"I'm going to go in and put it on right now," John declared.

"I will put on this sweater, but before we do," said Edmund, "I think Betsy should open her presents."

"Go on, then," Betsy said, and though she was dying to know what was in the pretty wrapped gift from Edmund, she reached for John's present first, which was wrapped in brown paper.

"Oh, John, that's the nicest material I ever saw! I will make a nice dress out of that, for sure. Some pretty."

"Now the pretty one, Mudder," George said, bringing her the fancy package Edmund had for her.

Betsy opened it, pulled out the item inside, and laid it on her lap. She folded the paper into a neat square and wound up the ribbon before picking up the gift again to have a good look.

"Oh, Edmund, this is beautiful. Thank you. It's some nice." She held it in the flat of her hand, its tiny stones sparkling and twinkling. It was a hair comb, but not like one she'd ever seen in a local store. It had pearls all around the flat part with white and green gemstones scattered throughout.

"Isn't that something, missus?" John said. "Look, 'tis green like the material for your dress. That's going to look right nice on you together. Sure, Edmund, I never even told you that, and you matched it up."

"I suppose everybody knows I likes green, I says it enough," Betsy said. "Look at you now, John Elliott, figuring out what matches me dress. You notices more than you lets on, old man," she kidded, pleased that he had.

"John is right. I didn't know about his fabric, but yes, I remembered you said green was your favourite colour."

"I'll wear this to church tonight even if my dress is brown, I likes it that much."

Betsy headed off to the bedroom to try the comb in her hair, fixing it in where most people would notice. It twinkled in the morning light, and she couldn't wait for Mervina Bailey to see it. It was the first pretty thing she owned that was hers and not something left by her mother-in-law. Unbidden, a tear came to her eye. There was something nice about having something that was all hers, all new, that nobody had ever owned before. She wished she could get more things that weren't part of somebody else.

"I never will, though, so long as I'm here, so I might as well wear this one a lot," Betsy said to herself in the mirror, leaving it in even though she was just cooking breakfast.

"Where's John gone?" she asked when she returned from her room.

"Outhouse. Betsy, when John said he was in the Waterford, was he—did he have some troubles or . . ."

"He had troubles, yes. He might still have 'em. They comes and goes. 'Tis nothing for you to worry about. The trip into the hospital might have shocked it all out of him."

"Oh. Well, if he's better . . . I just . . . he seems so well."

"He is, Edmund. Come on, I've got a big breakfast for me four men planned today. Going to fatten you all up! No talking about bad stuff on Christmas."

"Let me help. You tell me what to do, and I'll give you a hand," he offered, thinking she was always working at something. He and John were able to sit and yarn and listen to the bit of radio they could hear, but Betsy never stopped.

"Go on, don't be so foolish. Watch the boys and stay out of me way. I'll have it done before John gets back from the outhouse. Look at what George got done!"

Edmund turned to see that George had hooked the small boat that John had carved to the back of the train and was pushing it around. When John came in, he joined them, and before long the men were busy playing trains and boats on the floor while Betsy finished their breakfast.

The snow started up again with big fat flakes that fell straight down. Betsy didn't mind as long as it cleared away for church. She tapped the weather glass. It didn't look good. The barometer indicated it might get worse. Tired from their late Christmas Eve service that had ended just before the storm began, she figured there would be plenty of time over the twelve days to see everybody. It might be best if there was enough to keep away afternoon callers, she consoled herself. She watched John and Edmund play with the boys a moment before interrupting them.

"Come on, let's eat." She'd laid out a good breakfast for all hands, and they sat around the big table while she stoked the fire.

Betsy had bought extra oranges because she heard it prevented sickness, and since several children died of fevers every winter, she was an easy target for any proposed cure or prevention she could find. She put one beside every plate, all sliced up to eat with their morning meal. Then she started to prepare a black duck, two puffins, and four bull birds for dinner.

The wind whipped up stronger, bearing down on them from the northeast, bringing more snow. It worsened over the course of the day. The temperature dropped, and as the barometer indicated, the storm carried on with a ferocious rise in the wind. The gusts rattled the windows and shook the dishes in the cupboard. No one left the house, not even for church, and it wasn't much better on Boxing Day. Betsy lamented that they wouldn't see a visitor at all if the weather stayed so poor. Visiting at Christmas was the entire point of the twelve days, and to lose two of them would put a damper on the holiday.

They settled in to wait it out, expecting no knocks or requests for any mummers to be allowed in. John joked that more likely they'd all be asking to be allowed out because they'd be so desperate to leave the house by the time the storm abated.

Betsy rocked in her chair, disappointed about church but happy that they were all snug and warm. She watched John. His laughter was quick, and his hands were gentle as he picked up Richard. Her mind darted to her conversation with Edmund, and she saw him watching John, too. Edmund looked up at her and gave her a curious look, and she knew he wasn't satisfied with her answer. It was only a matter of time before he came asking again. She hated to talk about it because it reminded her of things she didn't want to remember.

For the moment, John was well, so she stuffed the worry down and smiled. Her hands felt strange to be doing nothing, not even holding a knitting needle, so she got up and walked over to the organ. She rarely played, but when she touched the keys, they were as familiar as always. Soon she was playing the old Christmas hymn "Silent Night" by ear. Betsy had taught herself to play, the first year she stayed in the Elliotts' house, as a gift to John's family for Christmas.

As she played, Edmund watched, thinking she played it better than anyone he'd ever heard. He wondered if there was anything Betsy wasn't good at.

NINE

Betsy's knitting needles savagely clacked against each other as the grey garment grew before her. Row after row it came into being, birthed onto her lap as she listened to the static-filled radio program that told of the happenings around the country.

The wind had died down long after sunset. The lamps offered just enough light to create a shadow from each of the three adults in the room. John read the *Twillingate Sun* paper, and Edmund studied a large book he had borrowed from Reverend Elliott, the Church of England minister, although neither man read much while the radio played. Betsy continued knitting the sweater for John, though the worsted chafed her fingers—new wool always did. Once completed, she'd unravel John's old sweater to create new sweaters for the boys. She looked forward to handling wool that softened and curled from previous use.

"The news is all about St. John's and the trouble with government," John grumbled, turning the knob to shut off the program.

"Well, St. John's is the only thing that matters to most," said Betsy, repeating a common refrain.

"True enough," John said. "They might be happy with our fish, but they don't care much for the fishermen."

"Ever think of moving to St. Johns, trying your hand at something besides fishing? When you were younger, I mean?" asked Edmund.

"Nah, always had the fish in me blood, b'y. Never wanted nothin' else."

"What about you, Betsy?"

The needles stopped for a moment. "What would I do in St. John's?" Betsy asked.

"Whatever you wanted to, I suppose, same as here. Raise your family."

"Betsy could have been whatever she wanted, but she's got it good here," John said, winking at his wife, who didn't look at him. The needles clicked again. Harder. Faster. The men resumed reading.

The beauty of the golden moon out the window shamed the kerosene lamp that glowed a pretty amber in the dimness of the parlour. It dropped to the islands on the far side of the bay, and the snow shimmered in its track. The cat, who'd worn himself out hunting the fat rats that lived underneath the cliff overhang in the little cove, scratched at the door. His belly full, he was ready for a warm hearth.

Betsy dropped her knitting to let King George inside. He scooted past her legs covered in white fluff, shaking as he made his way to the parlour. Though named after the current monarch by the late Mrs. Elliott, he sprawled in a non-royal manner in front of the fire to clean his damp fur. Betsy grabbed the broom to brush away the snow that had drifted in behind him. She paused mid-sweep.

"Is that a lynx?" she asked of a peculiar sound coming from outside. She'd heard lynx noises before, and they made several different calls, but this didn't sound like one of them. While the wild cats could sound eerily human, this was different. John and Edmund stood when

Betsy grabbed her coat and put her boots on. She listened again. "It's coming from the cove," she said. She sat to put on her boots and coat.

Haroooooo.

"Hear that?" Betsy hauled on her wool cap.

John heard the call, too, and had his coat and boots on in minutes. "Somebody's on the ice."

"Shipwreck?" Edmund asked, though he couldn't imagine a ship out now. Marine traffic lessened this time of year, and though it was too early for the ice floes, the cove had frozen solid these past two weeks. He put on his winter coat and boots and followed John and Betsy down the trail to the wharf. They moved to the left of the structure, where they could get on the ice and walk toward the sound.

"That's a man calling out," Betsy called back. "It's likely a sailor in trouble. You two get him. I'll go heat up some water."

* * * * *

Betsy returned to the house and stoked up the kitchen stove, then put a large pot of water on to boil, wondering what she would feed a stranger. She put the kettle next to it for hot tea and opened the tank to see how much warm water it held. A man on the ice would be cold and in need of food, perhaps water, warmth, and a place to sleep. The daybed in the kitchen would be a good bed, so she fluffed the pillow. Betsy hoped it was only one man. She would send Edmund for Julie if there were any injuries. She took bread and some cold rabbit meat from the pantry. Then, just in case, she pulled out bandages and salves and set them to the side in the hallway off the kitchen.

The wait wasn't long. Betsy saw the men coming up the path

through the window and rushed to open the door. Between them they supported a slight man whom they half walked, half dragged inside the house and over to the daybed, where he collapsed.

"He's fair froze," John said.

By the light of the lamps that Betsy had gathered into the kitchen, she studied the shivering man's pale face and thin clothes. Her orders came fast. "Undress him, quick. Get those quilts over him." The man's white face and blue lips concerned her. The men set to undressing him as Betsy rushed for another blanket.

"Frostbite?" This time it was Edmund who spoke. Betsy nodded, staring at the man's feet.

"Get a pan of snow," she demanded, hauling his legs off the couch. She rubbed his frozen legs downward to get the blood flowing, sticking his feet into the pan of cold snow when it arrived, knowing that if they warmed too fast, he'd be in terrible pain.

The man groaned. She kept rubbing his legs from knee to ankle, noting the angry red of the skin and the white around his toes.

"I think we can save his toes, but what of his fingers?"

"Fingers is red but not froze, Edmund. He'll keep 'em," said John.

"He's been too long out there, though, and he's in rough shape. Chilblains, and bad ones. I think the frostbite is mild. Here, wrap his feet with that old cloth there when I lifts them out of the pan." Betsy noted bloodstains on the man's right arm and wondered where they had come from, but she left the man to his secrets as she worked to wrap his feet, tucking his legs under the quilts. She cleared up the kitchen while the men dressed the stranger in some of John's clothes and wrapped a second blanket around him. His eyes opened, as blue as a summer's waters. He smiled his thanks.

"A bit of grub?" he questioned, and Betsy smiled back.

"Yes, b'y, I got that ready. You looks starved."

Their eyes met, and Betsy started. His stare was as cold as the frozen cove outside their house. She set about making up a plate for him and wondered if the chill had set him mad.

John didn't notice anything amiss and reassured the man that Betsy would bring him a fine fare with a hot cup of tea to wash it down. The man nodded his thanks again, and those cold blue eyes followed Betsy as she worked. She could feel them on her back, and she shook with the first shiver of that cold night.

"Here you go. You stay there. Pull up the chair, John, to put the plate on."

"Yes, missus, for sure." John helped the man sit up to eat and then pulled up a chair for himself. Edmund did the same. Betsy hovered around the kitchen, curious about the man's story.

"I was out hunting off New World Island, and my dory drifted when I lost the paddles. I left it when I got to the shore, seen your lights," he explained. His eyes flicked to Betsy and moored on hers for a long moment. Despite her curious nature, the young woman stood and left, unnerved by his surveillance. She shut the parlour door behind her and picked up a book to clear her troubled mind.

Later, while their visitor slept soundly on the daybed in the kitchen, Betsy climbed into her own bed and snuggled under the covers. She shivered, convinced that the coldness she saw in the man came less from the freezing temperatures outdoors than it did from something else. When John came to bed a short while later, she moved close to him, warm against his back, arm over his waist. Several hours later, she fell into a restless sleep.

T E N

"Another cup of tea, missus," Clyde Waugh ordered several days later. His name was a rare one, pronounced *wah*. He'd said he was from town and little else. He didn't sound like Paddy Bailey, though, and Betsy doubted he was even a Newfoundlander.

"The kettle is on the stove, and you can get it yourself. I'm tangled up with this sewing, and you're not lame," she retorted. His toes were in rough shape, but nothing that required the constant lazing about he did. He'd be gone now but for the deep cold that had set in, and high seas that followed the Christmas storm prevented a boat from even going down the tickle. To make matters worse, the roads were all still snowed in.

"Where I come from, the women listens when the man speaks," Waugh responded. "Now get me a cup of tea."

"I guarantee if I gets you that cup of tea, you'll wear it. This is my home, and we took you in like we'd take in any stray dog out there, but I'm not tending to a healthy grown man, and neither is Mary, so don't even start with her when she comes here next week."

"If you know what's good for *you*, you'd get it." Clyde Waugh remained on the daybed and watched her as she went about her work.

"If you knew what was good for *you*, you'd get out of me home and get back to these foolish women who does whatever you tells 'em," Betsy responded, with her back stiff and spite steaming from every pore. John needed to get the man out of the house or—swear to God—she would kill him.

The door swung open, and Edmund came in. He kicked his boots against the doorstop, knocked off the excess snow, then took the broom and swept what had made it in back out the door. He hung up his coat and crossed the kitchen to the stove.

"Don't get up, Betsy, I'll put the kettle on. John's finishing up and sent me on the way. How's the patient?"

"Fully recovered and lazy as the tomcat," Betsy said, shooting a look at Clyde Waugh, every ounce of hospitality gone from her.

Edmund laughed, but she was serious. He didn't like the man, either, and had noticed the way he ordered Betsy around, expecting her to do his bidding. Wherever the man came from, he had a different way of treating women than John Elliott or most of the other men here did. Betsy, for her part, resisted him at every turn, doing him no special favours.

"Well, that's good. John got extra work and could use a hand with it. Now, Betsy, I said I'd put on the kettle."

"Oh, I don't mind getting a cup of tea for you, Edmund, and for John. I'll get myself a cup, too. I think I'll take a break from the sewing and have a lunch. Maybe a nice bit of Christmas cake, too. We've got some left over."

"Got any more of that rum?" Waugh asked, irritated by her treatment of the others.

"Not a drop, and no more coming in the house until next Christmas. We Elliotts is not drinking people, and when what's bought for Christmas is gone, 'tis gone for the year." The young woman had another bottle stashed away, though. She'd hidden it in her dresser when she noted the gusto with which their new guest had guzzled the last one.

"I say your old man might have the last say in that," Waugh said, just as John threw open the door.

"Last say in what?" John asked, following Edmund's lead by sweeping away the snow he had tracked in.

"In whether more rum is brought for Christmas," Waugh replied. "Surely the missus don't decide that."

"Betsy is far smarter than me in those things, b'y. 'Tis a stupid man who marries a smart wife and pretends she's not. If she says there's to be no rum, there's to be no rum."

Triumphant, Betsy put cups on the table, one in front of John and Edmund, and one for herself. She set about filling the teapot, aware of the eyes on her back as she moved. She'd told John that Clyde had to leave, but John wanted him to wait until after Christmas. He agreed the man was hard to take, and Betsy bore the brunt of it, so he promised he'd keep him in the store loft in the daytime once he was fit, and now it appeared he was.

The tea poured, Waugh said, "What of mine?"

"Too lazy to haul yourself off the daybed, too sick to drink tea, I figures," Betsy said.

"Mrs. Parsons said to tell you to come over with the boys later for a bit of Christmas," Edmund said. He'd noticed the snap in Betsy's voice.

"Oh, you saw her?" Betsy picked up her teacup. She made a point of rolling her eyes to illustrate how much she was enjoying the hot beverage. Waugh's anger was tangible.

"No, she sent word by Walter," said John. "Mervina wants you over there, too. Paddy told me that when he brought back me wood plane."

"I'll go over after tea, then."

Betsy had done a lot of visiting once the weather cleared up. She'd seen her cousin Mary's family as well as other relatives and friends. She had helped deliver two babies, and both had lived and looked healthy and big, especially Mrs. Albert's. They had been overjoyed with the tiny clothes she'd made for the child, in particular a night-ie fashioned out of the cloth John had given her for Christmas. She could spare half a yard for a little girl baby to have a new nightdress. The second baby had been born to the Richard Elliott family. They had plenty and didn't need such gifts. They'd give the main midwife, Old Julie, some nice salt fish and a few turrs to repay her for assisting with the birth. Betsy took no pay herself, knowing Julie needed it far more than she did.

Clyde Waugh got up off the couch and made his way over to the table as soon as Betsy exited. The men were having a second cup and yarning, their days lazier than normal, given it was still the Christmas season and they'd overindulged a bit at Paddy Bailey's the previous night.

"Bailey might not be the most liked man in town, but he can make that accordion talk, swear to God," John declared.

"Mervina's got a lovely voice for singing, too," Edmund added.

"Good-looking woman, Mervina. Wish I could have a go at that," said Clyde.

"I don't think she's that kind of woman. She's pretty gone over Paddy, from what I can see," Edmund replied. Mervina Bailey doted on her husband and never gave any other man so much as a glance.

John remained quiet, studying Clyde Waugh. He finished his tea, then nodded to Edmund. The older man never worried about having Edmund in the house with Betsy, but this new man was starting to bother him. Sometimes men had weaknesses when it came to women, but that wasn't what he sensed from Waugh. He was more the taking kind, John suspected. Now he was starting to worry like Betsy.

"Ready?" Edmund asked their guest. "Come on, Waugh. Betsy says you're better, and you looked healthy on the rum at Bailey's last night. Sure, you can work on a few lobster lats for John to repay your board."

John nodded to Edmund, pleased that he'd spoken the words that John himself was too kind to speak. It appeared that not even polite Edmund much liked Clyde Waugh, and the mystery of where he'd come from was starting to plague John, too. Nobody they spoke to around the shore knew anything about him. Betsy disliked him intensely and wasn't up for hiding the fact. John would have to get him out the house, and hopefully out of the town, soon. Earle's boat might cross to New World Island after Old Christmas Day, and if so, he'd see that Waugh was on it, or they would be stuck with him until navigation reopened in the spring. If that happened, he couldn't guarantee that Betsy wouldn't end up killing the man before the winter ended.

ELEVEN

The lantern flickered orange and yellow against the dark tapestry wall-paper in the parlour. Some of the light spilled through the open door-way into the kitchen, but not quite far enough for Betsy to make it to the stove. She was guided by a path of warmth coming from it—easy enough to follow, given how the house still held a chill from the neigh-bours coming and going earlier. The weather remained decent enough for a stream of Christmas visitors and mummers that culminated on this last night, Old Christmas Day, with a full house. She hummed a song as she slid back the lid of the woodbox, felt for the wood inside, and pushed a junk into the stove. The rum had robbed John of his senses early on, and he'd stumbled to bed the moment the last visitor had left. Edmund and the other one—she refused to use his name—had argued politics until a short while ago. Edmund's voice had gotten louder and more frustrated as he listened to the man's insistence that the country should just give up and let England take over, or even join Canada or America as a province or state or some such foolishness.

Clyde Waugh aggravated their closest friends, Mervina and Pad-dy, though to be fair, Paddy Bailey could be as arrogant as their visitor when it came to politics. He was known to be a bit lazy, only showing up after the work was done. But a party, well, Paddy always showed up for one of those. A short time earlier, with a glance at Betsy, Edmund called it a night, and his foe had also retreated to his new accommodations, a small bed in the back room behind the kitchen. Betsy had set it up so that John could have his daybed back for daily snoozes.

The cat rubbed around Betsy's legs as she shoved another junk of wood into the stove and prodded it down with the black poker. The glow from the embers was her only light. Immersed in her duties, and her humming, the windows black as though painted with pitch, she had no time to react to the screech of the cat. A hand clapped across her mouth.

Betsy felt the heat of a body against hers. A hand fumbled and pulled up her skirt. She was forcibly turned around and pressed up against the cupboard, then bent over as another hand pulled against her clothes. She managed to manoeuvre the poker she was still holding and jabbed its fire-heated point against her assailant's forehead. The young woman turned on her assailant and held the weapon in front of her.

A feline howl filled the kitchen when Clyde Waugh stepped back, kicking at the cat whose tail he had stepped on. His face, a dark spectre, hovered in front of Betsy, and she wanted to jab the poker into his black eyeballs, her intense hatred for him hotter than the flames that flicked and licked at the chunks of wood she had poked into the fire.

He came at her again before she could try and grabbed her arm and twisted. A sharp pain shot through her wrist, and she felt the poker loosen in her hand. Before she could drop it, he halted his attack and let her go with a cry. She stumbled, surprised at her freedom, and retained the grip on her weapon. Waugh let out another harsh grunt, reaching behind himself like a madman, eyes stricken.

Over his shoulder, a pair of glowing lights appeared, and for a moment Betsy thought the devil himself had grabbed the son of a bitch.

Then she realized it was the cat, King George, his green eyes glowing in the dim light. He finished scaling Waugh's back, then hopped to the flat surface of the large warmer. The cat turned, arched, then hissed behind her left shoulder before sitting down and aiming his stare at the man who had stepped on him. He glared sentry-like from his post.

Betsy lifted the poker again. Her words, barely above a whisper, were strengthened by her anger.

"You will leave here tomorrow," she said. It took every ounce of her strength not to impale him with the poker. The clock ticked, marking off the seconds while Waugh debated his choices.

He slid along the back of the kitchen table, not taking his eyes off Betsy, who loomed before him, poker hoisted. His eyes adjusted until he could make out what she held in her hand. The pain of the wound on his forehead was increasing. He also noted the cat's eyes glowed a bright green in the firelight now flickering from the stove.

Clyde Waugh hated Betsy Elliott, the bitch. He had since the first moment he had set eyes on her, with her bossy ways and obvious displeasure with him. She'd not spoken one word to him tonight in the gathered crowd. With the party winding up, she had served food—offered it to everybody, even that jackass Paddy Bailey—but she never gave him any. Others had, but not her. Too high and mighty, she was. Needed to be knocked down a notch, she did. She looked at him like he was lower than the dirt, but he knew she'd come from the same type of crowd as him and just married into better.

His erection vanished. The searing pain had made him impotent for the night. He looked away from her glare and made his way to the back room. Once there, he found a scrub cloth and dunked it in an aluminum bucket of cold water to ease the pain from the wound. He'd get her back for daring to treat him that way. He fell into a dead sleep before he could plan how he would do so.

Once Waugh retreated, the cat jumped down from his perch and rubbed against Betsy's leg. It comforted her. She hurried to the parlour and shut its door behind her. Now with two doors between her and her attacker, her breath slowed, and her heart ceased to pound like rapid gunfire. She took a lantern from its shelf, carried it with her to the bedroom, and set it beside the bed. Her other hand still held the poker. Betsy set it down, not willing to return to the kitchen to hang it on the hook behind the stove where it belonged. She would find a way to explain it in the morning, if she needed to.

The bed sank beneath her weight, and she moved closer to the warmth of her husband's body. Safe in her room, it hit her how close she had come to being violated in the worst way. It shoved all thoughts but revenge from her mind. A hatred so intense that she didn't even start when the cat jumping on the bed replaced her fear. For the first time since she had picked him up as a kitten for Mrs. Elliott, King George slept next to the mistress of the house.

She petted and rubbed him to a purr as she drifted into a troubled sleep. The sound was a mark of contentment to the cat and a source of solace to Betsy.

TWELVE

Betsy seethed as she prepared a late breakfast for the men. Edmund was first to the kitchen.

"Edmund, it's you. Good. Sit down. Let me get your tea." Betsy's warm voice welcomed him. Delighted by the absence of a lecture for his behaviour the night before, he came forward with a large smile that hid his pounding headache, unaware her warmth toward him came from a place of relief that he was not Clyde.

Betsy flipped the toast on the rack over the open flame and gave it a thin skim of oleo, leaving two pieces dry and hard. Potatoes and bread dough sizzled in fat on the stove, and eggs had been hard-fried and stacked, two pulled to one side on the black sheet. The poker from the night before lay on an angle next to Betsy's plate. That's where Clyde Waugh's eyes went the moment he walked in, and Betsy noted his expression with satisfaction. She scooped up the bacon as John entered.

"Good morning," she greeted her husband.

"Well, this is a big breakfast for after Christmas," John remarked. His stomach recoiled a bit, but he'd eat or be killed by Betsy, so he sat down with fake enthusiasm.

"'Tis Sunday, John. Same breakfast as always on Sunday." There would be no church this morning, just an evensong service.

74

"Time gets all buggered up at Christmas. I lost track."

Betsy had risen early as usual and polished the stove until it gleamed, though it was not a Sunday job. She needed to busy herself. She had left the water from the cleaning chore in the pan, and it had cooled to a tepid grey with little bits of black floating in it. The men settled at the table, and Betsy divided the food onto the plates. With a sidelong glance behind her and a certain amount of stealth, she dipped several pieces of bacon into the grimy stove water. She took two plates and served John first, then set Edmund's before him with a smile that had the man's stomach doing somersaults for the second time that morning.

When she deposited Clyde Waugh's plate before him, without meeting his gaze—the food almost tipped off the side as she slid it toward him—Edmund perceived something was wrong. He noted Betsy's chair was closer to John's than usual and wondered at the poker on the table. Betsy never left things out of place. He noticed her glance from it to Clyde Waugh. Was that a bruise of sorts on Waugh's forehead? Edmund dropped his gaze when Clyde gave him a cold stare. Troubled by the tension, he nevertheless set to eating his breakfast.

"Some good, Betsy maid," John said.

"It is," Edmund concurred, slathering molasses onto a piece of toast.

John added pepper to his eggs.

"Not too much, now, we're low," Betsy advised her husband, her voice light.

Waugh wondered at her mood, but as he chewed the first bite of eggs and stared at the poker on the table, he understood. For the second time in less than twelve hours, Waugh felt tears sting his eyes. His tongue burned as his forehead had the night before.

"What happened to your head, b'y?" John asked, voicing the thought that was consuming Edmund.

Clyde swallowed the pepper-coated egg and washed it down with the cup of water in front of him. It wasn't until he had guzzled half of it that he tasted the salt. He struggled to keep the contents in his stomach as the realization hit him. Betsy had salted his drinking water.

Edmund watched dumbfounded as Waugh struggled for breath. He worked hard to compose himself, but he was struggling. Clyde moved the bacon around, hoping to find his voice, and took a bite of the cold meat with its odd smoky flavour and chewed. His nonchalance was a challenge, and Edmund knew it. John, however, was oblivious. His aging eyes couldn't read the nuances in the face of the man who sat opposite him at the far end of the table.

Waugh's voice was raspy, but at least the foul-tasting bacon calmed the heat in his throat.

"Poker last night," he said without further detail, wondering if Betsy would add some of her own.

"Looks like you fell on it," John remarked. "Betsy, can you get some salve for the man?"

"It's fine." Waugh looked stricken as Betsy jumped to get a balm for him. When she returned, he saw that she had put a dab on a small plate. She slid it across the table to him.

"It'll smart a little," she said, her eyes holding his. "But you're a man. You can handle it."

She returned to her eggs, and Edmund watched Waugh pretend to put some on his finger and dab the burn. Why was he afraid to use the ointment?

"Maybe you should let Betsy tend the fire, Clyde, b'y. So far she hasn't come close to burning her face off with the poker." John picked up a piece of bacon and chewed, closing his eyes to savour it.

Waugh picked at his food while the others ate with vigour. Suddenly a man so fond of his own voice had nothing to say. *Something's wrong*, Edmund thought, and it was big. Betsy was heaping revenge on Waugh, and there was a mark on his forehead. *What happened last night?*

The rest of the meal passed in relative silence, but when John suggested he and Edmund go get the boys from Old Julie's home, where they had spent the night, the fear that darted across Betsy's face and the look of satisfaction on Clyde's worried Edmund so much he declined. He suggested Waugh go instead, claiming writing work as his excuse.

Waugh looked angry but agreed with the plan. Both men, one filled up on a delicious breakfast he'd enjoyed despite his hangover, the other with a sickly lump of food he struggled to keep down, moved toward the door and were off in short order.

Betsy turned to Edmund. Her eyes filled with emotion, and he knew one of them was fear, the other relief. He moved toward her, troubled by the strange look on her face, and he caught her just before she hit the floor.

THIRTEEN

Later, after recovering from her faint, Betsy cleared up the breakfast dishes, clanking them one against the other as they swished in the water. The distant clicking of Edmund's typewriter punched the mid-morning's quiet. Mary had taken the boys with her to her parents' house after they returned from Old Julie's, and the opportunity for a rest was what Betsy needed and hoped for the minute the kitchen was shining again. The stovetop was smooth and silvery, and the peachy cream of the doors glistened. Her chores nearly complete, she stifled a yawn as she dried off the last of the plates and set them on the shelf.

Betsy heard Edmund's steps on the stairs and hesitated. The events of the previous evening left her feeling jittery, but she willed her hands to stop shaking and her voice to be steady. She figured that with a fainting spell this morning, she was getting as timid as Mervina Bailey. Next she'd be going on about her nerves being gone.

"Are you off to the store loft now?" she asked.

"What did he do?" Edmund's eyes drilled into hers. Most of the time he glanced down with some deference to her, intimidated. Now he looked concerned.

"What are you on about?"

Her brisk voice failed in its attempt to disarm him. "Waugh. You burned him with the poker, and you did something to his eggs." Edmund's eyes refused to drop.

"I did," she admitted.

"Did he . . . behave improper? Did he harm you?" The questions hung in the air. Edmund reddened, but he'd had to ask.

"He tried." Betsy dropped her eyes. "I can handle him."

"I've no doubt that you can." His voice dropped, softened. "But you shouldn't have to in your own house."

"Don't tell John. His sickness . . ." Betsy knew her husband and knew that such a thing like this might be what turned him to his weakness.

"*You* should."

"I should, yes, but I won't. Waugh will be gone soon enough."

"He should have been gone already. Damned boat needs to run. Are you feeling okay?" Edmund had been terrified when Betsy collapsed and tried to get her to call Julie, but she insisted that it had just been the heat in the kitchen.

"Oh, yes, I'm fine." She was growing another baby inside of her and had even felt it moving, but she couldn't tell Edmund such a thing.

His eyes wandered over her face, touching her forehead, her hair, glancing down her cheeks, and heat rose to her face and flushed her pallid skin. Edmund stepped forward and touched the back of his hand against her face. His touch was soft as he checked for fever, like she had done for her boys whenever they sneezed or looked a little bit sick.

No one had touched Betsy like that since her childhood. It jogged the memory of a man she hadn't pictured in her mind in years. With a desperate need to pull his face into focus, she closed her eyes. His image, as clear as though he had walked into the room, smiled. His eyes crinkled at the corners, and his dark skin, wrapped in a fisherman's web of creases and wrinkles that made him look so much older than he was, were warm. His familiar smile was on his lips, and a light shone from his dark chocolate eyes. Her father. She opened her eyes as Edmund removed his hand, leaving her face feeling cold and barren and craving more.

"You sure you're okay?"

Betsy pulled away, confused, and became angry. "I'm fine. Mind your own business," she snapped, much harder than she intended.

Edmund stepped back, realizing he had been too forward. He understood her anger.

"I shouldn't have . . . I'm sorry."

He stuffed his offending hands into his trouser pockets, then backed up and turned away from her. A second later he changed his mind and turned toward her again. Perhaps it was seeing her so vulnerable twice this morning that made him brave.

"But you're not all right, Betsy."

He used her given name for the first time. Betsy liked it, but her eyes flashed. Sometimes this man got right to her. She had been stoic all her life. It was the trait most admired and most desired, and being soft didn't suit this hard life. She worked and baked and sewed and did her duty. She had walked for water in the dry fall more than usual now, because there were two more men in the house. Betsy could handle the work just fine, but Waugh's advances had weakened her.

Shame, that age-old snake that coiled in the belly of a woman when she was mistreated, wrapped itself around her innards. Most men were gentlemen, she supposed. But not this one in her own home, the one who treated her like so much dirt. She cringed as she remembered his body against hers in the kitchen. Her stomach clenched and, God help her, she weakened even more and felt the darkness again. Before Edmund could process what was happening, she collapsed against him. She shuddered once before the sobs started—a silent shaking that he knew would embarrass a woman like Betsy.

Edmund wrapped his arms around her and held her close. Her hair was the scent of flour. His hands stroked her back and his voice soothed her as she wept against him. Moments later, she inhaled and pulled away from him, although his warm embrace and soft shirt were a comfort against her skin. She wanted to stay in his arms but resisted the temptation.

"I shouldn't be bawling like a baby. There's no point to it." She drew herself upright, rubbing a strong hand over her wet face.

"You're tough, Betsy, but I don't think any woman would be tough enough to be manhandled so. You shouldn't have to put up with that in your own home. Come on, tell John, or let me tell him."

"Edmund, look. You're not from here, but I am. I can't put me trouble off on anybody else, can I? Constable Sheppard is down to Fogo and can't get here, and they'd believe a man over me, anyway. Nobody believes a woman when it comes to this kind of thing. The woman always gets a bad name for it. Though nothing happened, there'd be those who would say it did. They'd look at me and wonder and say I asked for it, having two strange men in the house. Though I never wanted either one."

"I'm sorry I've put you out this winter, Betsy. I tried to keep to myself and not be much trouble."

"Oh, you're no trouble, Edmund. None at all. You listens good and don't make much work. You helps John, and I think that's keeping him happy this winter. Winters are not good on John. He has trouble with them. No, you're good as gold alongside the other fellow. He's the only trouble I got."

"I think you should tell John. He'll send Waugh away." Edmund was pleased she wasn't too put out by his presence. More than pleased, he was delighted. Coming from Betsy, the admission was high flattery.

"No, you're here, John's here, and I've got the poker. Plus, old King George will claw his eyes out if he comes after me again. But p'raps you could listen for word if Earle's is crossing? If we find out there's a trip, maybe you and John can make sure he's on it."

"Yes, I'll do that for sure. Are you sure I can't do more? I'll stay close, keep an eye on you, make sure you're not left alone with him."

Her shoulders loosened at his promise of protection.

"You're a good man, Edmund. You know, most of my life I knew nothing but good men. I got lucky, I suppose. Father was a saint, and so I expected saints and wasn't disappointed. First there was John, and now you. But the likes of Clyde Waugh, there's a few of them around, too, and that makes a woman's life hard."

"Maybe if I had a word with him he'd leave you alone." His helplessness didn't make him feel like a good man at all.

"Edmund, 'tis not that easy with a man like that. The Bible says we should reject every kind of evil, and I think he is pure wicked. The kind of bad you got to reject, not the kind you can fix. There's no light in his eyes. It's like he's got a devil in him, and I don't think he cares what you tells him."

"If he does something to you, I'll kill him myself," Edmund said with a flash of fury.

"You haven't got what it takes to do any kind of killing, Edmund, but I guarantee you that I do. It's good to have the nerve to do it so long as you don't ever have to. No, go on to work. There's nothing more to be said."

"Yes, I've got work to do. You're right. I'll take a bun to the room and a cup of tea, and like I said before, from now on I'll make sure you're not alone with him, ever."

Edmund set about making the tea himself. Betsy let him. She pulled herself upright, unaware she had been bent over. She heaved her shoulders back.

"Clean up your mess," she called over her shoulder as she headed to her room to use the chamber pot and sort out the wash. She bustled about as she listened to him rustling and fixing his food. Then he cleaned up his dishes. She let out a soft sigh when his footsteps drifted upstairs and not out the door.

Betsy walked to the kitchen, and the exhaustion that had plagued her for days overwhelmed her. She settled herself on John's daybed, closed her eyes, and fell asleep to the faint staccato sound of Edmund's typewriter.

It soothed her that he was in the house. Not just to keep her safe from Clyde Waugh, but because Edmund's presence made her happy for some reason.

FOURTEEN

Winter slammed down hard again that night against the saltbox at the edge of the cliff. It rattled the single-pane windows, and the house shook on its stilts. When it ended, the sun illuminated a new landscape. Snow piled in curling heaps underneath cliffs and flake stilts. The frozen cove sparkled with frost crystals in the glow of the morning light.

Mary had been with them when the storm hit, so she spent the night. In the morning, she lingered over her tea before leaving. The men went to repair damage on the property and gather for a yarn in John's store loft.

Betsy combed her hair and manipulated it into a perfect bun at the back of her head. Edmund's comb fitted in the top of it. She bundled up in her late mother-in-law's fur coat that hung past her knees. Her long, warm boots from New York City were too big but were stylish and peeked out from beneath the fur. Leaving Mary with the boys, she departed.

Mail had come before Christmas, and Mrs. Parsons had received a letter from her daughter Ida in Harbour Grace, which included a letter for Betsy. In Betsy's pocket was a letter to send back in the same envelope with her friend's mother's reply. Ida was older than Betsy, but they'd played cards together. Ida had often made up a foursome for card games at the house when she was younger, and now she was home on visits. As a young girl, Betsy had been fascinated by the older woman, who had gone away for a career and never married.

The walkway up to the house was cleared, the flat stone in front of it dry. She opened the door without knocking. Mrs. Parsons was sitting in a chair with her knitting, and her son, Walter, snoozed on the daybed. He awoke and grinned at Betsy.

"Where's John today?

"In the store loft. All the men are gone there for a yarn and to do a bit of work."

"Oh, that sounds like the place for me to be, then," Walter said. He got up and left in a hurry.

The serving girl took Betsy's coat and hung it on the hook where Walter's had been. A bit of snow flicked to the floor, but Mrs. Parsons laughed and told her not to worry about it. Her girl would wipe that up. Betsy could just come in and settle. Her tone was hushed, but the smile was genuine.

Betsy crossed the room to Mrs. Parsons and knelt beside her. The woman gave her a warm look, touched her face, and asked her to sit while the girl got the kettle going.

"I got a letter from Ida," the old lady said. She pulled it out from the pages of a book that sat on a small table beside her. Her memory was fading a bit at her age, and Betsy didn't bother to tell her she already knew. Mrs. Parsons handed it to Betsy, who read the first few lines.

"She's doing wonderful, that Ida. Off in Harbour Grace, teaching grown men."

Mrs. Parsons shook her head at the absurdity of it all, but in that gesture was also pride. The maid handed tea, hot and strong, to each of the women, along with a platter of bread, cake, and cheese. Betsy's eyes darted around the room. Her own house was similar in style and its equal in economics, and she always felt like she belonged here. They chatted about their Christmases, their families, and gossiped a bit. Time swept along in a most pleasant way.

* * * * *

In the store loft, the stove crackled as the men huddled around in a circle, rolling tobacco or puffing on their pipes. A skilled hand whittled some wood with a knife while another pair of hands mended a small cast net, and still another piled the wood near John in a neat stack from where it had toppled earlier. They worked on John's small chores, each knowing that they would get help with their own from the others, if needed. John's store was where they liked to gather, as had their fathers when it had been time to come together to do a bit of sit-down work. John had the radio and an insight into the happenings around the province that they loved to hear.

He also had the young man from Boston, whom they had their doubts about at the beginning. They figured he was soft and somewhat of an upstart, but they soon learned that, though he was book smart, he wasn't one of those who were just full of words and foolishness. He was also clever in ways common to men of the island, a resourcefulness borne of necessity that they acquired to keep them and their families from starving, freezing, or drowning, the three things that threatened them most.

On the other hand, the other fellow, Waugh, was a sleeveen. Sly, that's what he was, and quiet for a change. They nodded at his presence and forgot about him once the discussion heated to the same temperature as the pot-bellied stove.

"There's no goin' back, I s'pose. Now that the votes has been counted." John eyed the men, his expression shaded under heavy brows as he looked down at his handiwork. He carved with precision and care, watching his work closely when he could have completed the task blindfolded. He lowered his eyes to hide the shame that the political battle had been lost.

"No chance at all." The door had opened, letting in a draft, and with it Walter John Parsons. The men shifted over a bit. "That's it, boys. We got a new kind of government whether we like it or no." He leaned against a grey puncheon and folded his arms. Some work would show itself. He inhaled the scent of salt, fish, wood, and bark, like an elixir that stiffened the spine and strengthened one's spirit.

"Your missus is up over to the house," he said, nodding at John Elliott, and Edmund caught a grunt from Waugh as he shifted his leg, the first sound to come from the man who had been as still as night.

"A vote can't feed you, b'ys." John's words were met with nods.

"No, that it can't. But it can determine how you gets fed or if you do at all," Paddy Bailey answered.

The passion of the previous months had dwindled. In the first days when the announcement had come that responsible government would be traded off for a commission, the arguments raged. Physical blows were dealt when it became too personal, but like men do, when they all pulled a house across the ice, or shoved a skiff ashore, they figured out a way to move on from their differences.

Frederick Alderdice, empowered to run the country under the commission, was in charge. John had a serious feeling that this was the end of his country. He didn't know how or when, but he knew there would be no Newfoundland nation ever again.

"I had a dream," John said. The men leaned in with interest. Even Paddy Bailey held his tongue, for John's stories were always spellbinding.

"More than one, though. It first come upon me the night before the vote that ended it all. I went to bed, troubled, like we all were."

"'Tis not pleasant to watch the dissolution of your land," Paddy Bailey agreed.

"'Twas a strange dream, b'ys." He looked upward, remembering. "First, I saw all the money fade away, just vanish into thin air. Bills and coppers all faded to nothing. Right before my eyes, I saw it. I swear it was as real as you all are right here. Spectral coins and bills emblazoned with the word 'Newfoundland' disappearing into a fog. Then the stamps flew out of the post office and caught fire. They combusted into tiny flankers that swirled up and burned out. I never saw the like."

He took a breath and looked around the room at the men before he spoke again. "The Union Jack flag on every pole lifted up and flew into the sky, and I watched them rise and drift until I could see it no more. That has to be a sign of something."

"A sign you're getting old and foolish like meself," Walter John Parsons cracked.

"Oh, no doubt, my son," John laughed. "But old or not, 'twas a disturbing dream."

"Then what happened, John?" Edmund asked, wanting to hear the entire tale.

"I saw the schooners straining against their ropes until they burst forth. The rope ends were frayed as the ships drifted away from land and disappeared underneath the sea until all was bare. I saw all the symbols of a nation disappear over the course of the night. I tossed and turned, frightened to death. When I woke up, I got the news that democracy was all done in. Betsy cried. I never saw that woman cry before, and she tried to hide it, but I saw. I knew that if it made Betsy cry, 'twas bad."

John pushed a bit of tobacco into his pipe, not sure the story was over yet, and not sure it had even started. The dream was his own, a fabrication created by a restless mind. The reality was the real nightmare. Even now the dream recurred on occasion, and on those days after it first came, he didn't want to leave his bed for the heaviness of his body and his heart. He loved Newfoundland, and she was dying as a country. While others felt that it was a temporary measure, and many more didn't care as long as they didn't starve, John worried.

"Men from this shore fought for Europe." John's voice was clear in the shed, and the men leaned in again. "Back to a colony? Has any country ever surrendered their nation without a fight? Over there, they died for the kingdom, but they also died so the Hun wouldn't come for us. They *died* for England, and now is nobody willing to die for Newfoundland?"

"'Tis not the kind of battle you can fight with guns, is it, John?" Paddy Bailey asked.

"No, 'tis not. 'Tis a battle between the rich and us out here. The fishermen are at the mercy of the lot of them. But 'tis not fair to those who did fight. Young Aaron Porter, his mother looked for news for a year after he died in that field at Beaumont Hamel. Fred Roberts lost his arm. Do you remember that parade when he come home a year later? I do! We honoured him, but his eyes were not right for a long time after. Fred Waterman took a bullet in the back. Young Scammell from up in the cove—Walter John, you remembers him, he lived in your garden—he died over there the day the war ended. Countless Newfoundlanders was lost for the freedom of countries in Europe. And here we are, warm and comfortable with a democracy that we are handing away." He shook his head, disbelief etched on his face.

Edmund observed the men, who were looking at their work while smoking their baccy or chewing it. There was no reaction. All knew, and all felt their own regret.

"Well put, John, b'y," Walter John said. He uncrossed his arms and rubbed his hands together. "We just threw it away."

"A vote can't feed you, like you says, John. The commission will straighten it out, and we'll be back to a nation again," Henry Scammell said, his words meant to console.

"I don't know, b'y." John closed his eyes as though to think of his next words. The men waited for him to finish.

"Because that wasn't the worst part of the dream, b'y, not by far. It wasn't how the flankers flew on the breeze, and how the grey schooners with great masts drifted off the edge of the earth, that bothered me most. Nor the paper currency that had vanished into thin air. It was Father in a coffin. Just like the day we buried him. My father, who taught me that a country with a vote had the highest form of right and good government. He was in my dream, laid out just like I remembers, there in the parlour, in his best clothes, his face rugged and strong in the cold stillness of death. The lines in his dead skin were the tracks of a life lived hard and good. And covering his eyes was two big flat Newfoundland pennies—just like everyone else does to their dead. But his was different."

"Different how?" Henry Scammell whispered.

"They were melting. In the dream, them coppers began to melt, softening into globs of copper, then yellow like butter, and finally into pools of water. Them copper tears ran down through the wrinkles of the old man's face. I looked into the eyes of me dead father, who wept for a lost country, the nation of Newfoundland that was no more."

The store was quiet except for the snap of the fire.

"I don't think we'll be the country of Newfoundland ever again," John said, staring across the room at nothing in particular.

The men remained quiet as they set to work once more. While they busied their hands, they mourned for the country they were losing and felt the noose of guilt tightening around their necks. Each man knew that he could have done more to stop it.

FIFTEEN

Betsy breathed in the cold air and looked ahead. She had a good fifteen-minute walk ahead of her, a treat so rare that she slowed her normally brisk steps to savour it. The snow fell in big flakes as her boots crunched along the path. She pulled together the thoughts that raced through her mind and gave them her full attention.

Betsy resented Ida and felt guilty about it at the same time, because she loved the woman. Ida was brilliant and fun and kind. The thing that stirred these emotions in Betsy's was that Ida had gone away. Over twenty years she'd been gone now, off and on. Mrs. Parsons always talked of her with a longing that Betsy herself understood. Not just for missing the older woman, but because Ida was doing something both women had long wished for—living a life of adventure. For most women in the outports, going away was not a possibility. For women like Betsy, marriage was the optimal situation, but for a woman like Ida, there were other options.

Smart as she was, Ida was also beautiful and could have gotten a man, no doubt. The family money was doubly attractive to potential suitors, but that also made the difference in her choices. For Betsy, it would have been wonderful to have money of her own, to earn it herself. Sure, she poked a bit of money away, but it did belong to the family—she just had control over it. Of course, Ida would probably never have children. The woman was in her late thirties, and she wouldn't have that door open anymore, but it didn't seem like she minded much. Maybe children weren't her thing, anyway. She moved from town to town with the Advance Schools, a new initiative to teach grown men and women instead of youngsters.

Children are the hands by which we take hold of heaven, wrote Henry Ward Beecher. This was at odds with what the Bible said in the Book of Matthew, that "anyone who loves his father or mother more than Me is not worthy of Me."

Betsy believed the first and read the second verse many times to try to wind her way out of the trouble she was in, because there was no way she loved anybody, not even God, more than George and Richard. They became her whole reason for living the moment each had been placed in her arms, naked and squalling, with eyes as bright as the full moon and minds as swift as the north wind. She already loved the one that was starting to move around inside of her, and she hoped it was another boy. Betsy didn't want to watch a girl grow up, limited by the world and her situation, when a boy . . . well, he could do what he wanted if he got enough schooling and had half a mind to do it.

Deep in thought, Betsy walked past the store and glanced up to see movement through the window. She heard the low, deep buzz of the men's conversation within. Snow covered the path to her house, and she created fresh footprints to the front door. She slipped into the kitchen, staying quiet, as the boys were most certainly napping. Mary was nowhere to be seen. She leaned against the woodbox, removed her boots, and shook the snow off them.

The young woman walked in stockinged feet across the kitchen and put the kettle over the hottest part of the stove. She needed to get started on a supper of cold meat and bread. She baked every day now, Clyde Waugh making the difference for it to be a daily chore. Hatred for the man lived with her all the time and soured life in a way that she couldn't shake.

The door to the back room was open a crack, and light shone through. Mary should have put the tea on. Betsy glanced at the clock upon the shelf on the far wall and felt a moment of annoyance at the girl's neglect. A muffled cry came from the back, much like a child's whimper. Betsy stood, ramrod straight. Was it King George, the cat?

An odd clenching began in the pit of Betsy's stomach, a feeling she got when something wasn't as it was supposed to be. She scanned the kitchen, her sharp eyes taking in details she hadn't noticed in her effort to be quiet. The boots were her clue. They were placed just out of sight between the daybed and the stove, as though he had sat there and removed them and tucked them out of sight.

A violent pounding hit her temples, and Betsy realized it was her heartbeat. Heat crawled up her neck as anger built, bringing with it a rage that Betsy had only felt once before in her life, but that was enough to make her know it was appropriate to do what she did next. She pulled a large knife from where it was stuck in the wall and grabbed the great iron pan that hung by its handle from a nail not far away. Knife in her left hand, pan in her right, she walked to the door and slowly nudged it with her shoulder, every movement deliberate and stealthy, the plan in her head formulating in an instant as though she had thought it out for weeks.

She saw the bundle of skirt and the back of Clyde Waugh, who lay on top of Betsy's young cousin, Mary. So intent was he on his molestation he heard nothing. Her anger wasn't a wild thing—it was controlled. She walked up behind the man, who was intent on finishing what he had started, and raised her right hand.

The frying pan came down, *thwack*, over his head. He flopped prone on top of Mary.

Betsy saw Mary's eyes. Her shock was tangible, raw, and permanent, and her tears and terror mingled with pain and shame. Betsy hoisted the cast-iron pan again. *Thud. Thump. Crack.* Satisfied, she placed the knife and pan on a chair. With both hands she picked up Waugh's feet, heels toward the ceiling, and dragged his limp body off Mary.

Betsy didn't look at Mary, knowing the girl needed to cover herself. There was more to do. She lifted the frying pan again and whacked Clyde Waugh good and hard one more time. He wasn't dead—yet—but he was not coming to. A drop of blood seeped from the side of his scalp. His fingers twitched. Betsy tucked the knife under her arm, just in case.

King George sat on the stove warmer and licked his paws, unconcerned at the sight of his mistress dragging a man by his feet from the back pantry into the kitchen. The parlour door would be the best place to get him out of the house, Betsy figured, because out he was going. No homes backed onto the property on that end. She hauled the unconscious man into that room before going to fetch her boots. She had to get rid of him before Edmund and John came back.

A plan formed in her mind, and she grabbed Waugh's boots and decided to put them on his feet. She could hear Mary sobbing in the back room but ignored her. Betsy needed to deal with what was in front of her first.

Edmund walked into the house as she was carrying the boots

through. He took in Betsy's dishevelled appearance. She was carrying a knife and wearing her boots in the parlour. No one ever wore their boots in the parlour.

"Shut up and help and I'll tell you," she said before he could speak.

"Is he dead? Oh dear Lord, you've killed him, Betsy, haven't you?" Edmund's eyes grew round at the sight of Clyde Waugh sprawled face down in the parlour.

"Calm down, Edmund, just put his boot on," Betsy ordered. Edmund complied, his shock quieting him.

"My God, Betsy, what did you do to the man? Was he bothering you again?"

"Worse, Edmund. He was at young Mary." Her voice was calm, but even after such a violent display, her embarrassment at what she was saying came through.

Edmund, unlike Betsy, was unused to feeling anger, but he had grown attached to Mary, and his ire rose. Complicit now in the deed, he tugged the boot onto the unconscious man.

"I'm throwing him off the cliff," Betsy declared.

"So, he's not dead? I thought he was. We should try to get him to come to!"

"What? Save him? I wouldn't waste a dab of ointment on the likes of this. What odds? If we toss him off there, we'll say he walked off."

"No, Betsy, think about it. You could nurse him back now, if you stop. It's self-defence. But if you push him off the cliff, you'll be a murderer. You couldn't live with that."

"I could. I'm already over it. If you're not going to help, get out of the way." She grabbed the man by the feet again. Edmund noticed that Waugh's pants, though pulled up, were not buttoned.

"Dear Lord, help me," Edmund said as he picked the man up by the shoulders. He helped Betsy drag him outdoors and along a wooden walkway with a rail to help guide a man along to the outhouse at night. He saw the small building sitting near the edge of the cliff, and his entire brain screamed at how very wrong it was to toss a man like slop water from pails and piss-pots over the edge of a cliff.

Their unwieldy load never moved.

As they neared the outhouse, Betsy yanked Waugh's body off the wooden walkway and to the side of it, nearer the edge of the cliff.

"Put him down. He's a dead weight," she ordered, gasping for breath.

"Betsy, that's not funny," Edmund said.

"What? Oh, yes. Well, no, I s'pose not." But she laughed anyway.

It was at least a twenty-foot drop down to the landwash, where on warm days the ocean splashed away the slops thrown there and the waste that dropped from the outhouse. But in the winter, human waste sat rancid and stinking on the ballycater, a thin shield of ice covering the beach and adjoining the sea ice.

"His pants is open. They'll think he slipped on the way to the outhouse." Betsy kicked Waugh's shoulder, then shifted his body so his head was hanging over the edge.

"You won't be able to live with yourself if you do it, Betsy," Edmund warned.

"I can, and I will." She bent over to shove the man.

Edmund moved to stop her, but slipped. He fell headlong and struck up against the unconscious Waugh. It was just the extra shove the half-dead man needed to slip over the edge. Horrified, Edmund grabbed for Waugh's leg, but too late. The scoundrel slipped over and plunged down onto the waste-covered ice and rock below. He landed with a smack, his body contorted in a way that left no doubt that he was now indeed quite dead.

Betsy grabbed Edmund, who was at risk himself of slipping over the cliff, and hauled him back.

"Well, Edmund, b'y, you saved me the trouble, but now you're the one that's got to live with it."

"God help me, Betsy, I was trying to save him."

"If you wanted to save him, you would have done it in the house instead of helping me lug him down here. You just murdered him, and that's fine by me. Now come on, we got to figure out what to do about that. I had a plan, you know. I'm not stupid."

Betsy unlatched the door of the outhouse and left it open, looking at Edmund with something next to awe. "Jesus, b'y, you're more cold-blooded then you looks. Good for you."

"It was an accident, Betsy. Surely you know that."

"I saw you kick the man off onto the ballycater, that's all I knows."

He caught her eye and looked away, ashamed and taken aback by the look of admiration he caught in her glance.

"Come on. Let's go." The young woman turned toward the house, picking her steps with extra care on the snow-covered trail.

"We just leave him there?"

"You want to crawl into the slop to get a man that's already dead? Don't be foolish, Edmund. We'll make out he come down to use the outhouse and slipped. Stop thinking about yourself. We got to get Mary sorted. My God, how can you forget about Mary? She is only fifteen, and she's in pretty rough shape."

Betsy looked up at Edmund and grabbed him by the arms, shaking him. He saw something in her eyes that hadn't been there before. Fear. It shocked him. He didn't think Betsy was afraid of anything.

"We have to take care of Mary. Do you hear me, Edmund? What that man done to her? She's back there bleeding and crying all alone because of that bastard. You didn't see what I saw. If you had walked in when he was—my God, the look on the child's face. Do you understand what he did to her?"

"He—" Edmund couldn't say the words, but the horror of what the girl had just endured settled on him.

"Yes, he did. Look, let's just do one thing at a time." Betsy's voice cracked a bit, but she cleared her throat and went on. "Mary first, then everything else after that. You and me can help poor Mary, but only God or the devil can help Clyde Waugh now."

Edmund followed her to the house, his mind in turmoil. Was he a murderer? He *had* helped drag the man down there . . .

"Go get Old Julie for Mary," Betsy said. "Now, don't say much. Just say she's got a fever. The boys are still sleeping, but not for much longer."

"Yes, we must take care of Mary," Edmund agreed.

He *was* a murderer. He was going to hang. Betsy, too, probably, as she'd had a hand in it. In any event, he was sure Waugh had been alive when they had dragged him out of the house, and Edmund had been the one who had done the deed. His eyes filled with tears as he made his way to Old Julie's place.

Betsy proceeded through the parlour, glancing at the mess there but not seeing anything that couldn't wait to be cleaned. At least Waugh hadn't bled onto the floor. She made her way to the back room and to the girl.

Mary had not moved except to pull her skirt down. With a big scoop, Betsy picked her up, strengthened by the excitement of the moment. She carried the small girl to the parlour and tucked her under some blankets with soothing sounds. Mary's silence soon changed to sobbing cries as she settled into warm feathers and quilts. Betsy got up to get cold water to clean the blood off her hands—that of Mary, not Clyde Waugh.

The kettle shook, and she cursed herself and attempted to pour the hot water a second time. Anger and fear coursed through her veins, and a cold shiver of reality poured through her, reminding her that she had, with Edmund's help, killed a man. Sadness for the loss of Mary's innocence in such a violent way, relief that both she and Mary were safe from further violation, and a deep fear that there would be dire consequences all filtered through her senses, creating an anxious feeling in her heart.

But one thing she didn't feel, in her jumble of emotions, was remorse. She was, no matter how badly she felt in every other way, not one bit sorry that Clyde Waugh was as dead as a beach rock.

SIXTEEN

John's face was red from working in the heat of the store loft. He stumbled over the boots and gave them a nudge to one side as he sat on the chair.

"Who's here, missus?"

"Young Mary caught a bit of fever. Old Julie's taking a look at her." Betsy didn't look up as she cut chunks of potatoes and salt beef left over from the earlier meal into a pan of hot pork fat to make up a hash for their supper.

John shrugged and looked at the boys. "Keep them away from her," he said, his fear of fever always present.

"Where's Waugh?" he asked Edmund, who sat playing cat's cradle with George near the fireplace. John took the chair opposite and watched them as they figured out their moves.

"Thought he was with you," Betsy said.

"Gone to the outhouse, I suppose," said Edmund.

"Fell down the hole, I dare say, he's been gone that long," Betsy said from the kitchen. The nonchalant line fell from her lips as easily as her next words. "I'll see how Mary is."

The boys' room was dark, the blinds drawn, and Mary slept. Her soft, peaceful breath in the warm room was at odds with the trauma she had endured. Julie worked at the wash basin, cleaning the blood from the cloths she had used to take care of Mary's wounds. Betsy brought her another bucket of cold water, and Julie nodded for her to set it down next to the stand. Cold took out bloodstains best, so Julie dropped the rags in there. The pale pink water in the aluminum pan nearby drew Betsy's eyes. She shook her head.

"She was hurt bad, poor mite," said Julie. "I'll give her something to bring on her time." Julie had a concoction she made to help women when they needed a bit of a start in their menses. Her mother was American and had shown her how to grow bugbane. Women some-times came to see her when they were trying to avoid having another child. Having youngsters killed a lot of women, and sometimes it was better to stop one than have a brood left alone when their mother died.

"I don't think he finished up, but she was too shy to say much. I described what that would be like, and she didn't think that it hap-pened," Julie said.

Betsy averted her eyes, embarrassed by the description, though she had two sons of her own and carried another child. Old Julie had brought her first two into the world.

"No, I think I stopped him in time."

"Where is he?" Julie wondered how Betsy had gotten him out of the house without him having a go at her. She was just a girl herself, and while she was strong, not many women were a match for a man determined to have his way with them.

"I drove him out. He never come back."

"If you killed him, I wouldn't tell," Julie said, her pupils large in the dim light. She glanced at young Mary. "Me first husband, it's what he done. He caught me down in the root cellar getting vegetables, and he had me on the dirt floor. After, he always done what he wanted, and I had to marry him. Best day of my life was when that schooner hove in the tickle and I was told he was buried on the Labrador after fallin' from the mast. Boat was out of salt, so he couldn't be packed in it to bring him home. He was some hard on me."

"I didn't know that." Betsy knew that Julie's husband had died in Labrador, but these details were news to her.

"Well, I got me youngsters out of him, and he was dead before he could make his boys like him." Julie's sons were two of the finest young men around.

"I made up the parlour for her," Betsy said after a long silence. "I'll send Edmund over to tell her mother she's sick and keep her with me till she is better."

"Keep her here at least a week, maid. She's tore a lot. She's such a small girl. But I let her know she can have babies. Poor t'ing hardly didn't know how you got babies yet. She said she wouldn't have babies if it was so bad puttin' 'em in. I said it didn't always hurt that much, but I can't say 'twas ever nice."

"The right man can make it nice, Julie maid." Betsy blushed, and Julie flashed her a quick smile.

Yes, Betsy was one who would like it as much as a man would, Julie thought. Lots of women did, and she was right. Most of those women had nice men. John Elliott was as nice as they came. He'd walked Julie home a few times before she had been caught in the cellar and was forced to marry. Old Julie was only forty-eight, but life had added twenty years to her appearance. She was called Old Julie only because her first child was named after her mother and was known as Young Julie.

Supper sizzled on the stove when Betsy returned to the kitchen. She hauled out the bread and started to slice it as John turned off the large radio.

"You missed the broadcast, missus." He never knew Betsy not to listen while she made supper. "The young maid all right?"

"She's got a fever. Old Julie said she should not go home for a week. Edmund, you'll go over and tell her crowd after you eats?"

Edmund met her eyes across the room, and he gave a brief nod. He looked at the book he was reading, but the words blurred on the page.

SEVENTEEN

It was one of those sparkling nights where the nearly full moon dangled in the sky, bright and big. The cove was frozen over, and the large flakes that fell throughout the latter part of the day had left the entire area covered in a blanket of white glitter.

John glanced out the window. "'Tis some funny where Waugh is."

"He wandered in off the ice. P'raps he wandered back out," Betsy suggested.

Edmund and Betsy looked at each other. They knew John was going to want to go look for him. It had been hours.

Edmund tried to change the subject. "You read in the paper today about the all-star game? They're going to raise a bit of money for Bailey? They'll be hosting it in Toronto in February. The Leafs against all the best of the other teams. Should be good, hey?"

"Yes, b'y, I was the one that told you that. Will be a good game, and the Leafs will win it. He didn't say he was going somewhere else after the outhouse, did he, missus?" John would not be deterred.

"Never heard him say a word," Betsy replied in a hard voice.

"Me either," Edmund echoed.

John had his boots on before their words hit his ears.

"Come on, Edmund, b'y, let's go see if we can find him."

"Where to?"

"Outhouse first, to see if he fell in the hole." John winked at Betsy, "He must have went over to the Scammells' or the Parsons place for his supper. But he should have told you. Of course, that was more for us, eh b'y?" John nudged Edmund in the shoulder with his mitted fist, and Edmund forced a grin and a nod.

The walkway was covered again, though Edmund could make out a faint outline of where they had dragged Waugh from the parlour door to where they had thrown him off. He and John walked through the feathery snow as an idea took shape. Edmund walked faster and passed the older man. He stepped onto the walkway first. Grabbing the rail, he made as though he was slipping. He slid down and called out a warning to John.

"Bit slippery there, b'y," he lied.

While he felt a great deal of remorse after pushing a man to his death, Betsy had convinced him after a good row in the parlour that it served no purpose to go before the magistrate about it. His nerves were raw as he played innocent. He opened the unlatched door to the outhouse and made a big show of looking down the two holes. One of Waugh's feet was visible, but Edmund ignored it. It was well past dusk, and he wouldn't be expected to see much in that light.

Outside, however, John could see the outline of a man. He hollered to Edmund. The curtain moved up at the house, and Edmund saw Betsy's face in the window. The moon slipped behind a cloud, and everything went black for a moment. Edmund took advantage of it to take a deep breath to calm himself and pretend he couldn't see.

"Where?"

"He's down there, b'y, on the rocks. Dead as a doornail, I imagine."

"Is he? Are you sure? I'm not going down there." He couldn't, under any circumstance, have any part in retrieving that body.

"We needs to see if he's alive at all, but I don't know how to go about it. I can't reach with the gaff. I suppose I could go up the slope and come down on the beach and walk across the ice."

"Don't be foolish. It's slippery as hell, and the ballycater might not hold you," Edmund warned. It alarmed him that John might go and get himself killed trying to figure out if Waugh was dead. "Let's ask Betsy what to do. Another few minutes won't make a difference. That man is most assuredly dead—nobody could survive that fall—and he's been missing a long time."

John did not relish the idea of edging out on the ballycater in the dark. He didn't like dealing with a corpse, either. Furthermore, he certainly didn't want to be crawling around under the outhouse.

"Yes, Betsy will know," he said, relieved at the suggestion.

Betsy waited at the door.

"We found him, maid. It looks like he slipped on the walkway and is down on the rocks. Must be twenty feet down and is surely dead," John relayed to his wife.

"Oh my." Betsy put her hand to her chest, and Edmund marvelled at how very shocked she looked. She could have been on stage with one of those fine actresses in Boston who entertained him and the Taylors on Friday nights at the theatre.

"I nearly slipped myself," Edmund said, falling in line with the charade. "Could have been killed."

"Oh, thank goodness you didn't. Is he down in the . . . sewage?" Betsy cleaned up her question at the last moment in respect for the dead.

"Yes, maid, fell right into it, I allows. I think he's dead."

"He headed there right when I come back from visiting Mrs. Parsons. He's been on those rocks all day, he must be."

"Yes, he must be," Edmund agreed.

"We got to check," John said.

"Well, you're not going traipsing around those rocks tonight, John Elliott. Young Edmund, I don't want you down there, either." Betsy had deliberately thrown in the word "young" to make sure he understood who was in charge. He might have kicked the body off the walkway, and he might be several years older than her, but he was a terrible liar. She didn't want him to have to answer any questions.

"No, I s'pose that would be stupid," said John. "He is dead. But I got to get some of the men to come with me to check, maid. P'raps some of the others has an idea."

"I'll stay with Betsy," Edmund said. "It's a bit much for a woman to have a dead body by the house."

"Yes," John said, realizing that this would upset the women, especially Mary, who was suffering with a fever. John felt a bit of sadness. That Waugh, he wasn't the kind you took to much. Worked good enough, never caused much trouble, but not particularly likeable. These thoughts plagued his mind as he made his way over the hill to the Scammells' to see if they could lend a hand in the extraction of Clyde Waugh.

Betsy looked to Edmund. "Come on, let's go into the parlour. I'll have to tell Old Julie about Waugh being found, but she's still in there with Mary with the door shut. Now, don't give me that look, Edmund. We're doing the right thing here by letting this be an accident. Come on."

Edmund followed, still reeling from the events of the day, too rattled to do much more than follow Betsy's lead.

* * * * *

They were still in the parlour when Old Julie brought the enamel pail to the kitchen. She had heard Betsy in the parlour talking with either Edmund or John—she couldn't make out who—and so, slipping her boots on, she let herself out the door. There was too much blood in the water to toss in the snowbank, and the herbs Julie had given Mary had cleaned the girl's bowels, so the pail was full.

The moon lit her way, and as she approached the outhouse, she saw the trodden snow near the edge of the cliff and took a peek over. Instantly, she spotted Waugh's prone figure below.

"Jesus. She did kill him," Old Julie said. "You done the right thing, my dear. That's where *you* belong," she told the corpse of Clyde Waugh, and damned if she'd tell anybody. He deserved to rot on the rocks, the dirty bastard.

Julie remembered her purpose then, and an idea darkened her thoughts.

"Perhaps a bit of a douse wouldn't be a bad idea. Warm you up a bit," she said to the body below. She removed the cover from the white enamel bucket and flung it over the cliff onto the dead man.

She placed the lid back on the pail and walked back up to the house. When she returned, Betsy and whomever she was arguing with—sounded like Edmund—were still in the parlour. Old Julie decided not to tell them what she'd seen, decided to leave the entire thing to unfold, and pretend she had noticed nothing in the darkness of the night.

EIGHTEEN

Early the next morning, a group of men walked across the cove with gaffs and fished Waugh's body from beneath the outhouse. He was covered in "sewage," as Betsy called it. Knowing there was nothing to be done, and that the body stank too much for anybody's fine parlour, they took him to the stage. Old Julie came to them later that afternoon.

"He was in some state, Julie, and none of it washed away because it's all froze up, and he still stunk. S'pose at least the body couldn't get washed away," John said.

"Now, get on with you all, I been doing up bodies for a long time," Julie told him and the others, kicking them out.

Outside, the men breathed the fresh air, glad to be free of the odour wafting from the corpse.

"Reverend Elliott still away?" Henry Scammell asked.

"Yes. Not sure when he'll get back," John said. "I suppose we could get the Salvation Army man or the Methodist fellow. I am the lay reader, so I could bury him if I have to."

"'Tis cold. We could lay him out in somebody's store somewhere until the minister comes back."

"Well, he can't be laid out in a parlour, Henry. Do any of you want that stink in your store?"

The men all shook their heads.

"I don't think we got much choice but to bury him right away," Edmund said. So far, nobody had brought up the constable. People died here all the time, and the constable was in Fogo. He could probably get up with everything frozen over on that side of the island, but nobody would bother him for an accident.

"Look," Edmund said, deciding it was best for him and Betsy if the man was buried sooner rather than later. "We don't even know what church he belonged to, so likely whatever graveyard he goes in, he's sure to be in the wrong one."

"You got a point," John replied. "What if we buried him up in the garden in the old plot?" There was an old graveyard with about ten of John's relatives' headstones. They were the first settlers before the churches started, and there was space there.

"Should we get a telegram off to the minister to see what's to be done?" Henry asked.

John stared off, his breath a white mist in the air, his heart troubled by a man with nothing, nobody, and no place to be buried at the end of his life. "I don't think we need to. We got to take care of this ourselves. If they don't like it, they can take it up with me. We'll have a time digging a hole, so we'll need as many hands as we can get. Bring sharp axes. The ground is froze solid. Father always said dying in winter was a big inconvenience, and I can't argue with that."

* * * * *

Julie stared at the corpse on the table, her hand over her nose. The stench had nothing to do with decomposition—there was no way he had rotted overnight, especially in the cold temperatures. She'd hit him dead-on with her bucket of slops.

"Well, you old son of a bitch, you sure ended up right where you deserved to, didn't you, ya old bastard? Not much to you now. You're all stiff, but that thing you used to hurt that poor youngster is as floppy as a capelin, and not so big. I'm supposed to clean you up, but I think the shower I give you last night is plenty of washing for the likes of you."

Faced once more with Waugh's body, she dipped a bucket on a rope down through the trunk hole and into the hole sawed in the ice below to draw up some salt water. Thinking the men might hear, she made as though to wash the body. Instead, she tossed bucket after bucket of water onto the roughly hewn wooden floorboards of the old fish stage and used not one drop to wipe the rapist's body.

She left him as he deserved to be—unwashed, pants hanging open, dead penis the size of a thole-pin exposed in the cold air. She used a gaff handle to push the stiff body into the pine box sitting across the two woodhorses. He landed on his back with a thud. She had already hauled out the nice satin wrap the men had gathered to line it and folded it into her bag. There was better use for that. Instead, she stuffed brin bags from the pile in the corner of the stage around the body. The burlap's rough texture scraped against his pale, clammy flesh. Then she hammered the lid on the box.

When her deed was done, Julie called John and Edmund back in.

"I couldn't do much with the smell. Can't soap him up good here with cold water. And you'll never get it out of the house if you takes him inside. You know, I heard he was a Catholic, so you might not want to put him in one of our Protestant graveyards."

"Catholic?" asked John. "P'raps we should get Paddy Bailey over. He'd know what to do with a Catholic."

"Paddy's off to Fogo. Not back for a day or two," Edmund said.

"Is that right, now? Well, that settles that. No Catholic priests around this place. We were thinking of burying him up in the garden, and now I'm sure that's the right spot for him. We knew nothing about him and he never told us much, even when we asked."

"Oh, yes, I knows his crowd, and they don't like that," Julie lied, determined to have him buried in unconsecrated ground. "If his family comes, they'll be right upset. I wouldn't put him too close to your crowd. Just up alongside. Dig a hole there and put him down. I'll send off a telegram and let them know, and if they comes for him, they can move him home to his own graveyard."

"We never knew where he come from and didn't know you did, Julie. Yes, that sounds like the right thing," John said, now fully satisfied that they were doing the right thing.

NINETEEN

There was big talk that a man had fallen to his death at the Elliott outhouse, but nobody suspected anything more than an accident. Clyde Waugh had garnered a reputation for being a disagreeable sort, so no fuss was made when they lugged his box off to be buried alongside John's old people in his upper garden. Julie had told everyone that the man should be buried immediately, that there was a terrible smell already coming from the dead man, and it would be unbearable in another day or two. It was like that with some dead bodies, she told everyone—they immediately begin to rot and stink something fierce. There was no reason not to believe her. Old Julie knew all kinds of things about dead bodies.

The smell still lingered after they dug the hole and put the box in.

"Seems wrong to bury a fellar without a proper funeral," John Elliott said, looking down the hole at the box.

"Needs a prayer, at least," Edmund's uncle Garland Hoffe said.

"I'll start. Our Father, who art in Heaven . . ." John Elliott began speaking the only prayer to be said in his deep island dialect. The few people standing there bowed their heads. He read some of the service for the dead but didn't bother with the entire thing.

"Ashes to ashes, dust to dust." John threw some snow and dirt down. They would get the minister, Reverend Elliott—no relation—to say a proper prayer as soon as he got back, if he thought it was needed.

The snow and dirt gave the mixture a marbled effect as they tamped it down tight with their shovels.

"Feels like we should do more," said Mark Hart. He was new to the island, over from Port Albert and married to a local girl.

"Well, we're not Roman Catholic," Walter John Parsons said, leaning on his shovel. "If we was, we'd have a big wake for him."

The men looked at the grave. Hart grinned and said, "Well, 'tis a sin not to have a wake for a good Catholic boy. A good drop of rum won't do any of us any harm?"

Edmund spoke up. "Not at the house. There's a sick girl there." He looked at John, who nodded.

"S'pose we could do it in the store loft, have a drink to a poor dead fellow, have a wake all proper like. He's after dyin', so s'pose we should do that much?"

The men fell in with John's plan, heaved shovels over shoulders, and walked home to meet back at John's Cove.

After a while, with the stove lit, the men sat back with their donations of homebrew and leftover Christmas rum. It wouldn't be a tear or anything, just a chat and a memorial to the man they barely knew.

"Well, so we should pay tribute to this fellow, I s'pose." Walter John raised his glass. "John, did you come to know anything about him? Everyone says he kept to himself a lot."

"He showed up one night. It was a hellish storm. He was half froze to death, so we put him up. Got to put up a man who comes in off the ice. He never said who he was, but Julie just told me she knew his crowd, that he was Papist. Not sure why she never said nothing about knowing his crowd before. She sent a telegram off to them."

"Never knows what kind of trouble a fellow might bring . . ." Mark Hart trailed off, and the men who were ten strong now looked at him, waiting.

"Well, b'ys, you know I've been away down to Fogo. Just got back two days ago that calm morning we had. So, I never heard about this fellow being around. I'm not sure if it's the same fellow, but I remembers a story told to me by a fellow who was from down the bay. The more I thinks about it, the more I thinks this might be your man Waugh, though that wasn't the name I was told. And it wasn't a good story, either."

John gave Mark a piercing look.

Mark tossed a cigarette in the snowbank, where it fizzled out. "Not right to talk bad of the dead, and I could be wrong."

"Yes, not right at all," Edmund said, not wanting to hear what the man had to say. The rest of the men leaned in, though.

"Well, he was a hardcase. You know Jim Boyd, right? Over around the bay?" Mark asked.

The men nodded. Jim Boyd was well-known. He had several boats and a large family, and he fished on the Labrador with them each spring.

"Well, word is this man got at one of Jim's daughters. Just thirteen, she was, and Jim found out. All his b'ys shoved Waugh—if it was him—in the punt and dragged the punt off, then put him out on one of the islands and left him. That was some time before Christmas. Suppose this could have been the island they left him on. They didn't leave the punt."

"You can't be at a young maid—or any woman." This was spoken with venom by one of the men and seconded by all.

"I waited for Betsy until she was eighteen before I married her." John's voice was calm. His quick mind moved to young Mary, now settled into the parlour while she recovered from her fever. "Are you thinking that dead man is the same as was put off on the island? And he made his way here? How would he last this long on an island with no food or water?"

"S'pose he crossed on the ice and got up on the south end. He might have holed up in the lighthouse, I s'pose. They keeps a bit of grub up there," said Mark.

"Well, I don't know how he come to be here," said John, "but if he's that bad, I'm not gonna wake him."

"Well, might be all lies, b'y," said Mark. "You knows people talks."

"It might be all lies," Edmund echoed. The knot in his stomach grew tighter, and he tried to loosen it with the rum. John looked closely at him.

"Well, I'll drink to him," said Dolphie Brinson, raising his whisky flask. "Because if he was buggering with young girls like that, he is right where he's supposed to be, smellin' like shit and buried in the ground."

The men, one by one, slowly raised a glass and drank.

John kept his eyes on Edmund. He threw back his rum and said no more. His suspicions needed no answering. The man was gone and the girl had a fever. That was good enough for him.

The men, made gloomy from the talk, departed and tottered off to their homes shortly thereafter. Edmund and John walked to the house with its yellow light glowing from a lamp lit early for Betsy as she worked.

In companionable silence they came upon the front step, and as Edmund reached for the metal latch to open the door, John put a hand on his shoulder and gently patted it.

He knows, thought Edmund. *He knows.*

TWENTY

Julie cleaned Mary and put more bandages between her legs. The child whimpered at the recollection more than the pain.

"She's asleep now. She's got an infection. I think she'll heal, but she'll never get over it." Old Julie shook her head and put on her coat. Betsy nodded. She knew without being told that Mary would always remember the violation.

Edmund walked into the kitchen as Old Julie left. John had objected to her walking home alone in the dark and was walking with her. Edmund's tension festered like a blister about to burst. Betsy sensed it and motioned to the table.

"Sit."

He obeyed, pressing his forehead into the palms of his hands.

"Everybody's gone now," she said. "Mary and the boys are asleep, and you're dying to say stuff, so just say it." She had no time for his foolishness. What was done was done. Betsy was sick of looking at his face, which was sadder than poor Mary's these past couple days.

Edmund looked at the table as he spoke. "They says Waugh was at a girl up around the bay and that's why he was here."

"He was hiding?"

"Well, yes, I suppose. Not even sure that's his name, though Julie says she knows his people. Look, Betsy, you know I didn't want to cause a man harm, don't you?"

"That fellar never did nothing but harm. He's burning in hell, where he belongs."

"He smelled some bad. I thought we missed the pile of—"

"Old Julie emptied the slop kettle over him."

"What?"

"When we were in the parlour. I saw her. I happened to be looking when she heaved the slops over the cliff."

"Why didn't you tell me that? Oh my God, so you think she knows it wasn't an accident? You should have told me!"

"I'm telling you now. You were frightened to death. And Old Julie only knows he was dead and nothing else. She didn't know we knew when she spotted him. Calm down, my son. You're going to be sick if you don't stop it. And she never said anything, so that makes her as guilty as we is, anyway."

"God." He raked a hand through his hair. "I suppose you're right. I can't sleep for thinking about it."

"If you hadn't accidentally shoved him, I would have. Did you think we were dragging him off to make snow angels?"

"I don't know what I was thinking. You said to do it, and I just—I don't know. You don't have any remorse?"

"Remorse? You mean am I sorry he died in a shit pile and is buried in the dirt?" Betsy's laugh at such a silly notion made Edmund a bit sick.

"My God, Betsy, I'll go to hell. I have to talk to the minister."

"Don't you dare be talking to the minister. Are you out of your mind?" Betsy's eyes flashed. Her hand came down on the table hard.

Edmund twitched at the sound, his nerves rattled. "He'll send a telegram straight off to Constable Sheppard. He don't keep secrets from the law. He'll be up from Fogo and haul us both off. Then who will take care of the boys? Mary?"

"I know, I know." Edmund's stomach clenched. "What about going to hell? Aren't you afraid?"

"I'm going, anyway, if that's where you go, I figures," she yelled, then quickly put her finger to her lips, listening for sounds from Mary or the boys. Edmund followed her stare and then met her eyes when she was satisfied.

"Look, the way I figures it, we probably saved another girl or perhaps more from the trouble he was doing to Mary. If he did it before, then he was probably going to be at more girls. He was a young man, and there are a lot who we saved. If we sit tight, we'll get away with it. Nobody cares about Clyde Waugh."

"Look, I know he did it to you, but that doesn't condone—"

"Tried." Betsy closed the conversation with just one word. She glanced at the poker.

"You sure he didn't do it to you, too?"

"No, Edmund. I'm a married woman. I knows what men does, and I can fight off a man." She grinned at him. "And puss helped. That cat, he's better than a dog. He near clawed the face off Clyde Waugh."

Edmund laughed, though he wasn't ready to find it funny. He felt like a cold-blooded killer. "I'm going to have to live with it, I suppose."

Betsy knew Edmund was soft and sentimental. She walked up behind him and hesitated for just a moment, then placed her hand on his back, the same way John had comforted him. Edmund had the brief thought that John and Betsy were better matched than they looked. Each one was able to celebrate the death of a man a bit better than him. But the stroking of Betsy's hand, warm through the light shirt he wore, distracted him. He felt more than comfort and more than a desire for her. He held his breath as her hand touched his strong shoulder.

As much as she thought of him as young, Edmund had become very strong and very much a man under the workload he carried. This experience would toughen him up more. His soft life in Boston and St. John's would be buried under the darkness found in this spot of the world, where perfection and imperfection were soulmates.

Betsy pondered the thought of a mature Edmund, thinking that his ideals were something to be admired. And she did appreciate them, but they wouldn't help him survive long if he followed them too closely in this land. Her hand drifted along his back and touched the hair at the nape of his neck, and he exhaled. It had grown long in the months he had lived with them, and it tickled her fingers.

She heard his breath quicken and brought herself up short, realized the intimacy of what she was doing.

"Let's not hear no more talk of this. Mary is to be tended to, and if this got out, it would ruin the girl. Think of somebody other than yourself, Edmund." Betsy's harshness covered up her softer feelings, and Edmund blushed at his silly thoughts of Betsy liking him in the way a woman liked a man.

"Yes, I know. I will think of Mary." Edmund fell quiet and resisted an overwhelming desire to kiss Betsy. He didn't quite know why her approval was so important to him, and he felt whiplashed as he was pulled back to the reality that she didn't like him all that much after all.

He would never be hard like the men she admired, though from what he could see, they were as good as him. He'd always followed the rules. They did, too. The difference was they made the rules themselves in this hard land, and sometimes they had to revise them for the sake of survival. This set him apart, but he couldn't help but wonder, if he were a bit more of their way, would he get more of Betsy's respect? Gaining it had somehow become his strange and impossible goal.

TWENTY-ONE

"Thanks for coming, Miss Sharpe. Thank you for helping Mary. We are delighted that she did so well this year." Betsy walked the Church of England teacher to the door. Mary had refused to go back to school after the fever left. Her face had been pained, and tears flowed when Betsy broached the topic.

"Please, Betsy, let me stay here. I can't face them. I know they don't know, but I knows, and I can't see anybody," Mary had implored, hands covering her shame-filled face.

"Oh my, Mary, I'll see what I can do." She wanted to tell the girl to smarten up, to move on, but something about her beseeching eyes had stopped her from being her normal gruff self. It was then Betsy had gone to see Mary's teacher, and upon learning that Mary had done most of her work already that year, she convinced Miss Sharpe to give Mary her exams early, and at home, because of her fever.

"I'll miss her in school," the schoolteacher said after delivering Mary's exam's, all corrected. "She's a star pupil. I'll write up her report card. She's got top marks going in, so I don't think we've much to worry about." The teacher's lips trembled. She really liked Mary and was pleased to help, but she would miss the sweet girl who worked hard and had such a bright mind.

Betsy had already spoken to Mary's mother, who really didn't have much time for her, anyway, with another baby on the way and two other daughters to help. She also had a secret hope that the Boston fella would take to Mary, and, well, like most people, she listened to Betsy when she made a suggestion. She hadn't been told the truth of the situation, at Mary's request, and certainly didn't want the fever in her house.

Before the assault by Clyde Waugh, Mary's eyes always had a certain brightness, despite the hardship at home and her shy ways. Some of it came from being chosen by the Elliotts to help, as well as the kindness with which they treated her, allowing her to stay many days when she wasn't needed at home. Some of it was genetic, having sprung from the same tough clan as Betsy. That light returned after her exams were completed. Perhaps, thought Betsy, the studying and preparation had momentarily relieved her mind of the awful thing that had happened to her.

Edmund came into the parlour. The younger girl's smile and the glow in her eyes flashed even brighter.

"You're looking well, my love." Edmund still sounded softer in voice than most of the men. A touch of a Boston accent blurred his R's and gave him a bit of an elite air, though he looked more fisherman than scholar these days.

"I am." Mary lowered her eyes, then lifted them to Edmund's. "Thank you."

Edmund smiled back at her, and Mary drank in the warmth of it before he left them alone. Noting the exchange, it dawned on Betsy that perhaps her cousin fancied him. When he left the parlour, she sat with Mary while the boys played on the floor with a spinning top. She watched Mary sip her tea and dish up a spoonful of soup. The girl picked out the chunks of salt beef and chewed, savouring the salty taste.

"Now that exams are done, back to work with you. We needs our parlour back, and you can go back in your bed with the boys when you cleans up here. Time to get off your arse, Sally Anne." She softened the order with an affectionate smile, but she knew that being busy was better for healing than sulking and lying about. With her brain no longer filled with studying, and her body healed, household work would be good for her.

Mary nodded and glanced at the boys before speaking in a low voice. "You killed him good, Betsy. Thank you."

"Shhh now, he fell off the walkway," Betsy insisted.

"Yes." Mary offered a grim smile. "I don't know how people does that to have a baby, but I s'pose if you wants one bad enough, you does it. What was God thinking when he made us that way?"

"My dear, if you knew how often I wondered what God was thinking, you'd think I was fair heathen. I mean, did you ever look close at a sculpin? Ugliest fish you ever saw. What was that about?" Betsy winked, and Mary burst into laughter.

"I suppose I shouldn't question God. Do you think that, if I gets a husband, he'll care?"

"My dear, a man hardly knows much about women, so if you don't tell him, he'll never even notice. Whoever you ends up with will love you too much to think about that."

"Good. No need for him to know a thing, and I'm going to forget it meself. I have to figure out a job to do now that I finished school, make some money, perhaps. Or go to teacher college," Mary said.

The girl had grown up too fast and under the wrong circumstance, but she sounded tougher. Betsy thought that was better than being all soft in this day and age on the island.

"My God, Mary, you're some young maid, you are. You'll have a wonderful man sometime, and you'll forget all about this bit of trouble. Women have it hard sometimes, my love, but we can't be foolish about it. You are the best worker I've ever seen. You'll be just right for working with Old Julie with the babies someday, too. A girl as hardy as you, Mary, you'll be just fine. As for husbands, I expect you'll have a fine one in a few years."

Mary's eyes lit up like the child she had been, delighted by the great compliment paid by this woman who rarely doled them out and whom she admired more than any other. She would work hard to live up to Betsy's words, too. She would get a good husband by being a wife like Betsy.

"Everybody says you're the smartest, hardest-working woman on the island," Mary said.

"Oh?" Betsy had never known such a thing. "That's just old foolishness."

"Oh, I don't know. Mother and Father, Nan and Pop all says you're the best thing whatever come here, helping with the babies and taking care of folks, and also the way you runs this house and took care of old Mrs. Elliott till she died." She left out the part where folks said Betsy kept all Mrs. Elliott's belongings and didn't send any to her sister-in-law because, first off, Mary thought she deserved it, and second, it would ruin the good mood Betsy was in.

"Well, it's just what you does."

"Edmund, he knows?" Mary's voice was younger again, just for a moment.

"Oh, no, he don't know a thing," Betsy lied.

"Oh. I thought he might, since he come here after and helped."

"No," Betsy lied a second time. She knew Mary needed to believe the lie enough to accept it.

"He don't?"

"No. Men don't need to know women's business. Besides, they don't want to know."

It was best for Mary that as many people as possible thought she were still pure. It was also important for Mary to think people thought that. It wasn't the girl's fault, but that wouldn't change how people would look at her if they knew the truth. Luckily, she hadn't gotten caught with a baby, so the lie would be easier.

Mary got up then and pushed up her sleeves, like she often saw Betsy do. "Well, let me get at something." The entire time they talked, the boys had been playing in the kitchen. But the minute she got up, they scrambled in to her, and she picked up one and reached out a hand. "Let's go, boys." George grabbed hold, and with Richard propped on her hip, she left the parlour.

* * * * *

Edmund came back and discovered Mary fussing around the boys. Encouraged by his smile, she pulled out a chair for him, then fixed him a bite, taking charge of the kitchen the way Betsy always did.

Mary's decision to find herself a husband solidified. She figured if she had to have a husband, then it would be the gentlest man she knew, and that was Edmund. He wasn't like the men around here, who might be a bit rough in some ways, and Edmund, she felt, wouldn't ever hurt her. He would only bother her with that awful thing to get a baby and no other reason, and since she only wanted one or two babies, the most she would have to endure it was once or twice. She also considered that Edmund would be her escape. He was going back to Boston. Mary decided he must fall in love with her and take her when he did. If he needed more time to fall in love with her, she had another idea in mind.

She puttered around the kitchen and acted as wife-like as possible. Edmund noticed her new attitude.

"You look wonderful, Mary," he said in his earnest and honest way.

"Thank you, Edmund." Mary was pleased with how well it worked.

Later, when Betsy walked into the kitchen after hauling snow in to melt for water, she put the rest of her plan in motion.

"You're the best cook on the island. Everybody—even Mom—says. Can you teach me how you does it, Betsy?" Mary asked.

"Sure, maid, sure." The girl's compliment delighted Betsy. Mary could already do the basics, but she was taught by her mother, whom Betsy found had a bland hand and a habit of overcooking everything.

Betsy, too, had realized that the best thing would be for Mary to get married. There were lots of young men around. She warmed her hands over the stove. They stung like a thousand needles as the heat drew the frost from her skin. It was a good idea. A good cook would get a good husband.

She had no idea that the husband Mary hoped to take was Edmund.

TWENTY-TWO

The rocker squeaked in the darkness. Richard snuggled tighter, his face pale in the light of the lamp. George's fever was gone, and he slept in his mother's bed, tucked in beside his father for warmth. But this little fellow, Betsy's youngest, suckled at her breast again for the first time in weeks. Nothing there but comfort, and that was plenty for a sick child. She flinched a little, her breast sensitive with the pregnancy, and rocked a bit more. She hummed under her breath and stifled a yawn.

Footsteps sounded on the steps, and the cat lifted his head and looked beyond her, his green eyes two marbles of light in the darkened room. She continued her rocking, but the humming turned to a *shhh* as Edmund came around and reached for the lamp beside her. He turned the wick up just a little so he could see her better in the dark.

"I'll take him." His gentle voice reassured her as he stretched his arms out to the little boy of whom he had grown so fond.

Edmund, the only child in his family, had not been around children much and had no idea what to do with them or how to relate. The benefit was that he never even thought of it and spoke to them like little adults. The boys loved him for it, and he'd grown fonder of the two boys, who looked much like their father but in colouring possessed the dark snap of their mother with her black eyes and dark hair.

Richard stirred, but he didn't wake as he unlatched. By the glow of the light, Edmund caught sight of a breast, full and round over the top of Betsy's blouse, as he lifted him. Betsy didn't notice him blushing, and for that he was grateful.

It triggered a memory of a night back in Boston.

He opened the door to the chambermaid. A touch of her hand and he was aroused, and she pushed him back into his room. The wick on the lamp had been high, the light bright because he had been studying. By that same glow the girl leaned back on his bed so that her legs bent and her feet touched the floor. The flickers of light illuminated the dark hair between her thighs as she spread her legs for him, her hands holding the fabric in bunches and her eyes with a daring look as he crossed the room, dropping his trousers and stepping out of them.

It was over in about a minute. He couldn't meet her eyes, but she kissed the top of his head and whispered, "All right for a girl like me, but your poor wife will be disappointed one day." He blushed and moved away from her. "You've not had a woman before? Yes, you're only a boy. How old?"

"Seventeen," he whispered.

"Well, you just need practice," she said primly, pulling her skirt down "I'll give you practice, for a cost."

Edmund gulped and nodded.

"You're young, sure. We can practice again in a short bit."

"All right, then."

A while later, coins safely tucked in a little purse, she took off all her clothes. It took short work for Edmund to be ready for his practice, and the next time was a longer lesson. When he was done, she directed his hand to her.

He was an eager student, and she came to him frequently, a drain on the bit of pocket change he earned, but paper and pencils were all he really needed, so he spent a few pennies on the maid, and she, in turn, was able to feed her family well.

The unbidden memory, the maid's name long forgotten, dissipated as he tucked the little boy in his bed, a tiny figure all alone in the dip of a feather mattress. Betsy still rocked in her chair when he returned to the room. He stood in front of her and she rose, the chair coming to a halt in the dim room. Her hair hung in strands around her face. He couldn't see the dark circles under her eyes or feel the weariness in her bones but knew they were both there.

He reached a hand out and touched her shoulder. A fondness crossed his heart, a caring that was unfamiliar and had nothing to do with the glimpse of her bare body. He pulled her into an embrace, a brotherly move. She melted against him, his warmth a solace to her aching shoulders. The child inside her moved a little, but she ignored it, and it wasn't enough for him to feel.

Edmund wanted to care for this woman, who was able to care for herself just fine. He meant to let her go, but her lips came up to his, and he returned the kiss with no thought. Desire darted through him, and he wanted her more than he'd ever wanted anything in his life.

Her cold lips hardly knew what to do, so unfamiliar was this passion. Just when Edmund felt he would die for wanting more, Betsy pulled away and backed up. Regret filled her as she backed away. She wanted to stay, ached to stay, but instead she turned and walked toward her room.

Edmund sank into the chair. What had he done? He allowed the horror to slip over him and roll down his body in a wave. What had this place turned him into? A murderer and an adulterer—or whatever they called a man who touched another man's wife.

He would have to go back to Boston early. He wasn't ready to leave yet, but there was no doubt that after his behaviour, Betsy would make him go. Edmund scraped a hand through his hair, tension interfering with his thoughts. He picked up the lantern and made his way upstairs. There was no point in losing sleep over it. If he had learned anything these past months, it was that worry was a useless thing. He'd face her wrath in the morning after a good night's rest.

TWENTY-THREE

Mervina Bailey came by the next morning. A fully healed Richard and George played with little Charlie Bailey and Edmund in the parlour. The door rested open so the heat could be shared with the kitchen. Edmund thanked God the visitor shielded him from Betsy's anger.

Betsy kneaded dough at the table, cursing herself for not having done it earlier. Exhausted, with both boys having fevers and fussing all evening, she'd slept late. Then there had been that business with Edmund.

Young Mary had gone home to help her mother with the new baby that Betsy and Old Julie delivered a few days before. Betsy's fist hammered the dough with a smack.

"I knew you were the murdering kind," Mervina said.

Edmund stopped mid-sentence as he was telling a story to the boys. A rushing sound filled his ears.

Betsy halted her assault on the bread. "What do you mean?" she asked, her voice sharp.

"Trying to kill it, maid?" Mervina Bailey laughed, nodding toward the dough, spreading the copy of the paper out on the table before her. She glanced at her boy. Charlie was robust and happy.

"No, I just want to get it all done. I'm late starting this morning." She met Edmund's eyes above little George's head and gave him a sober grin. He exhaled the breath he hadn't realized he'd been holding.

Betsy laid the pan of dough on the warmer to rise. She washed her hands and dried them on her apron. Then she brought the teapot over to the table, refilled Mervina's cup, and poured one for herself.

"We got some milk from the Strongs now, and we gives it to the boy. You got yours, too?" Mervina asked.

"Yes. You want some in your tea?"

"No, I still likes the tinned milk in my tea, maid."

"I do, too, but the fresh milk is some good for drinking."

Betsy nodded in the direction of the pan of dough on the stove and said, "We been using the brown flour again, too. Not nearly so nice to look at, but I think I like it better. We took some up the island to Reynold's Cove for the crowd up there, told them about the beriberi and that the white flour was the problem."

"What did they say? Folks on the dole isn't always good about learning new things."

"I told them it was in the paper. I told them of the two men up on New World Island who ended up unable to walk because of it and that they had weak legs. I said 'tis all we uses and we had extra, and we do. Before Mrs. Elliott died, she only wanted the white, but now I'm stocked up on the brown. I give them a sack and told them to mix it with the white they already got. Oh, and my, was it ever cold there. I could hardly bear it. I knows the old man can't cut the wood, as his legs is weak, and perhaps he already got the beriberi, right? But still. It's poverty, that's what it is. I hope the flour works."

Mervina sucked in her breath and read the report of Dr. Parsons in the *Twillingate Sun* again. She and Betsy had little in common, one stoic and stubborn, the other rather silly and loud. People wondered at their friendship at all, but there was no real mystery. They had one thing in common—a great determination to keep their children alive—and unlike the families they'd been born into, their situations afforded them the money to do so. They swore by cod-liver oil, even though their children hated it. But down their throats it went while others skipped the pungent stuff and dismissed its health values. They both urged their husbands to get cows for milk, but in the meantime, they settled for purchasing it from John Strong, who had many farm animals down in Morey's Harbour and was willing to sell it to them for their boys. They had both read Dr. Parsons's report on the scourge of beriberi, a disease caused by lack of vitamin B, and given up the fluffy textured white bread for the old-fashioned brown.

Edmund held two-year-old Richard on his lap while George and Charlie Bailey played in front of him. Mervina's boy looked much like the other two. Young Charles Bailey was just three years old but could speak better than the older Elliott son. This was not surprising, since his father loved the sound of his own voice like a sailor does a foghorn in a raging storm near a dangerous shoal.

Charles's large, expressive, dark blue eyes were full of life and mischief, and he held Edmund spellbound with his adult questions.

"If a plane comes on the tickle, will it go through the ice?"

The door swung open. Edmund started, and young George Elliott careened over to his lap to hold his leg while Richard popped a thumb in his mouth, a habit he couldn't break no matter how often his mother put rum on it. In fact, John suggested they stop using that remedy, concerned the child might become a raging drunk because he liked the taste so much.

"I've already told you all about the planes," Paddy Bailey boomed, his voice an irritation to all, including his ever-patient wife, who was tired of her blowhard husband and his need to take over any and all conversations.

"Good day, Paddy," Edmund said, standing and taking the youngest boy up in his arms.

"Sure, you'll make him sooky picking him up all the time," Paddy said. "Can't be makin' boys sooky." He rubbed the hair on his son's head, so unlike his own ginger waves.

Mervina sipped her tea, subdued by her husband and embarrassed by his display. He always took over, and she was used to ignoring the eye-rolling and lack of respect the men of the town exhibited for her husband. Betsy stifled a grin as she rose.

"A cup of tea, Betsy," his voice boomed, though she was already on the way. "So, John's not here? I come to talk about the situation with Clyde Waugh."

The teakettle clanked against the stove, and Edmund's heart raced. Paddy hadn't come to help bury him, because he was off to Fogo. Even so, as John had said, if Paddy had been around, he'd have been too busy writing letters to people in St. John's, who likely didn't want to read them, offering to help out when he was needed.

"What about him?" Betsy snapped.

"Well, he needs a proper burial, b'y. Now, I heard the man was dead, but I was tangled up with business and couldn't help. I only just learned he was Catholic from Mark Hart. Now, a good Papal lad needs a good service. I think we should get him up and send him on the next boat to his people."

"You want to dig him up?" Edmund's heart pounded as he sat back down and released Richard.

"Oh, yes, it's only right. We don't want a good Catholic fellow going off to purgatory, now."

Edmund recoiled. "Well, I'm not going to be part of digging up a man." Murder aside, that box was rancid.

"He wouldn't have been put down in the ground so fast if I had been in on it. Far be it from me to ever do something halfway, even though me poor mother thinks I'm doomed since I gone Church of England, but I don't think a Papist should be buried up in the garden like a suicide. Sure, he should be sent to his own people. If I had been here—I'm not sure why the men didn't come and get me, Edgar . . ." He conveniently forgot he was in Fogo during the burial. "No way would a good Catholic boy have been in the ground in unconsecrated land like some crook," he carried on. "He's baptized into the church and should have a churchyard, for sure." He pulled in a long breath, then, his barrel chest heaving and his lungs dragging for air.

Paddy often vacillated between buffoon and blowhard, his views coming out one after the other at breakneck speed. It was as though he was fearful that if someone slid one syllable of sense into the thin gap between the words of his rants, they might shine a light on the illogic of them. Most of the time there was no logic, just an overblown vanity that had most of the men either excluding him or laughing at his expense. Often, one or the other did a mock performance of the man, using some of his favourite expressions, like *far be it from me to say* or

I couldn't care less, which he splattered throughout his soliloquies like fly spit on a fish flake in August.

"His name is *Edmund,* not Edgar!" Betsy told him from the kitchen.

Edmund, baffled by Betsy's lack of anger about his actions the night before, was shocked by her further defence of him. "I don't know. I think that it was the best that could have been done, and you were in Fogo," he said with a sidelong glance at Betsy. This Bailey fellow was hard on his nerves at the best of times.

Before Bailey could respond, Betsy spoke up. Her eyes flashed as she handed the cup to him. He stood about a foot taller than any man in the town, and she wondered—having never been there herself —if all the men from St. John's were this tall.

"So, you're all for diggin' him up, now, are you?"

Even Paddy had the good sense not to get Betsy riled up. He had not, as of yet, been at the edge of her tongue. Something, perhaps an instinct of self-preservation, told him that she could rip him to shreds in that department. The idea of a woman dealing that kind of blow to his ego kept him reined in whenever he was in her presence.

"Well, I think his family would have wanted it that way—"

"The man is in the ground for his crowd to come get him," Betsy interrupted. "He is safe and sound there, and here we are in January with ice froze in and the ground froze over. You knows 'tis a hard time to die in the winter, and the gravediggers can't even keep up on our own. There was no 'front to that fellar, to his people, or to his church. I suppose putting him inside the Church of England cemetery would have been just as insulting to a Catholic, but that man never told us he even had people anywhere. All we knows about him come out after he was dead.

"I say the best thing for you to do is to write a letter to his people over in the bay and tell them to come and get him in the spring, if you're so big on the letter-writing and all, and so good at it. When it's done, you bring it to me, and I'll send it off myself for you, stamp and all." She didn't mention the rumour about Clyde Waugh having hurt that girl up in the bay or that his name might not even be Waugh, though she supposed he would have already heard about that.

Edmund marvelled at Betsy's brilliance. Paddy Bailey spent a good portion of his time writing letters to politicians and newspapers. He fancied himself an expert in politics, and being from St. John's, he felt he was superior in his ability to voice the concerns of the island to the important people there. Every now and then one made it into print, and most often the recipients of the letters would, out of politeness, draft him a reply, which he would hoist proudly and talk about incessantly. He always took it as a sign of his importance, not only in his own community but in that paragon of unequalled value, St. John's. Of course, most of the time the editors just needed to fill space, and his letters fit the gap. And given his stinginess, Betsy's offer to pay for the stamp would for sure be accepted.

Paddy took a deep breath. "Well, I did write that letter to Mr. Smallwood, but he never wrote me back. I thought first when he come out talking on the radio that he might have been a good man to be involved in a lot of stuff. He talks a good talk. I heard him in there, giving a speech, but I don't say he'll amount to much after all. No, not answering my letter is a sign that he won't go far. I don't see much of a future for him. Now, I suppose I just need to keep writing to the crowd up in Botwood about getting a runway built here."

"When was the plane in Botwood, Uncle Edmund?" Paddy's son asked.

But Paddy was quick to jump in, not wanting to give Edmund, who was garnering a certain amount of respect in the town, the satisfaction of answering Charlie.

"Mr. Lindbergh landed in Botwood last summer. He would have landed here if it was winter because we have the tickle, and we could have cleared it off like we've been doing for planes when the first one landed here in 1921 with the mail. That was in March, and before I came here, or else I would have written a letter then and got a proper landing strip in. I didn't get told about Mr. Lindbergh's journey to Botwood, or I would have told him to come here instead. Perhaps we could have built a landing strip up on Big Marsh for the plane to land in July, but that wasn't told to me. People didn't get him here, but at least this was the place the first air mail came to, so we are in history that way. Too bad, though. I'm sure I could have gotten Charles Lindbergh here instead of him going to Botwood if I had been informed."

Betsy and Edmund's eyes met as the young boy gave up on getting a good story about airplanes. Paddy droned on until his tea sat tepid in his cup, a fact he complained about, though it was his own chatting that had kept him from sipping it while it was hot. Betsy resisted the urge to say that and made him a new cup. She invited the whole family to stay for dinner, something that surprised John Elliott when he came in, as Betsy could barely tolerate the Bailey patriarch. He had no way of knowing that she was making sure that the entire topic of digging up a corpse was removed completely and fully by planting a number of other distractions into the man's brain.

By the time Paddy Bailey harnessed up the horse and crunched over the snow in the bright afternoon sun, he had a head full of people to whom he would have to write letters. His wife and son sat on a plank between the two seats of the sled, huddled in a blanket, his words whistling by them. There were declarations about the government, radio announcers, roads and coastal boats, and most of all, that Joey Smallwood fellow, whom he was certain by the time they got to their saltbox house in Main Tickle would never ever amount to much in life whatsoever.

TWENTY-FOUR

Betsy pinned her hair tight to her head. Still, wisps of fine, curly growth that always accompanied a new baby escaped at her temples and neck. Her waves frizzed in the heat of the kitchen, her hair being the only thing in her life that tended to defy her. The morning had been relentless, as had all the mornings of the month. She fought to stir the fires in both the kitchen and the parlour, working hard to keep them going as the chimneys devoured the flames like mammoth dragons that hurried the burning of wood junks. John and Edmund harnessed the horse early each day and disappeared for hours, having a boil-up in the woods most days. This meant a late cooked supper that had her cleaning up well into the night. But the stack of wood along the path kept growing, creating a railing of sorts as it was replenished.

Early mornings tired her as she cooked a good breakfast before they set off. She was tempted to nap each day when the boys did but resisted, having too much to do for such a luxury. The boys were stricken with cabin fever, which made them contrary, and Mary came only on Mondays again. Her test results had been astounding—top marks despite her Mondays working with Betsy and her time off during her troubles. The extra days in Betsy's parlour had paid off, and now that she had turned sixteen, Mary had a definite maturity about her. She was considering going to teachers' college in the fall in St. John's, an ambition Betsy encouraged more than her parents did. Her mind full of dreams for her young cousin, she didn't hear the scratch-rattle of the horse and sleds coming up the garden until they were just outside the door.

Curious, she leaned closer to the window as Edmund tied the pony to the clothesline pole. She wondered why he and John hadn't put the mare away before coming in. Betsy's heart did a little flutter of concern.

"What happened?" she asked her husband as he came inside.

She glanced at the children, her first thought going to the many who were ailing in the community. Childhood was a difficult stage to pass through, and as many people under ten died here as over fifty. However, an old person wasn't likely to send the two men out of the woods early like this, unless it was family. John's blue eyes were dark like the winter sky. There was loss in them, and she caught her breath, knowing that his words were going to be painful. Betsy braced for them.

"There is bad news, missus. Terrible bad news."

Edmund removed his double-knit mitts and set them carefully on the shelf where Betsy always told him.

"There was a terrible fire over in Harbour Grace . . ." John took a breath, and in that span her quick mind travelled to it.

"Ida?" Betsy lifted her hand to her throat. Her heart thumped in her chest, and her other hand found the back of a chair.

"She didn't make it out. It was the entire block where she lived, I hear. A telegram was brought over to the Parsonses by Evelyn Hynes this morning. They're in an awful tear over there, my dear. It's a sad thing. We run into Charles Scammell. Pretty tore up, he was."

Edmund watched Betsy's face as a wave of emotion washed over her. In an instant he saw horror and shock turn into grief, and then, with a shake and a shudder and one quick sob, she looked squarely at them and said, "This is a sad thing, but 'tis not ours. We turn ourselves to their needs now."

John nodded. Edmund copied the gesture, and the men waited in silence for her to speak, both grateful for her lack of hysteria. Neither would have dealt well with that.

"I suppose you don't know more than that?"

"Just knows it was a fire and that the poor woman died. Was in the middle of the night."

"She would have been asleep. She wouldn't have even known," Edmund offered.

"You knows that?"

"I figures it's most likely."

"I wonder if that's what got the goat all worked up," John said.

"The goat?" asked Edmund.

"Ida's goat?" asked Betsy.

"Ida's got a pet goat, Edmund," John said. "The animal went crazy, got out of the pen and got into the house. Nobody knows how he managed to do that or why, but Walter John told me about it. Was quite a goin'-on."

"Not proper to be telling funny stories now, John," Betsy admonished.

"Was funny then. Not sure anymore."

The men pulled their grub box out and handed it to Betsy.

"We began to eat but didn't finish it," said John. "We came home when young Scammell told us the news. Figured you should know."

Betsy was grateful for the task, something to occupy her as the air around her thickened. The sound of the boys playing and the men being overly quiet all pushed against her. Her mind separated from her soul in a way that hadn't happened since her little brother Frank died of influenza. That time she had floated above her grief, unable to shake it but unwilling to give in and contribute to that empty look in her mother's eyes by reminding her of it. She had been six and wise enough to know that the only thing worse than a your own grief was seeing the grief of someone you love. Betsy would be strong. She always had been, and so she would again.

TWENTY-FIVE

On Sunday evening they attended evensong, but it was not a regular service. Edmund sat at the end of the Elliott pew with the two boys. John did not attend but instead had gone without a word to his bedroom and hadn't come out, not even for supper.

Betsy sat looking forward as the rector entered the pulpit in his flowing robes. The dark golden wood of the altar glistened, and the church was packed. The elderly matron of the Parsons family was there, and a whisper of sympathy for her spread through the arches of the wooden church. There were murmurs of admiration for a lady of such an advanced age who had her well-loved daughter snatched from her by such tragic circumstances.

The hall silenced, and the evensong service began. The only sounds were the turning of prayer book pages and the voice of Reverend Elliott as he followed the course of the service through its pages. The words of the rector filled the giant hall. His echoes were silenced, and the resonance of his thunderous but soothing voice was absorbed into the wool, fur, and cotton of the coat-bedecked congregation on this bitterly cold Sunday evening.

As he spoke, giving praise to a woman who deserved as much as any minister could heap upon one, Betsy's heart began to pound against her chest, and the warm coat she had kept close around her now caged her. The ease with which she had killed Clyde Waugh consumed her thoughts.

She would not be deserving of high praise when her time came to be remembered in this cold building. The crowds would not remember her with the same fondness as they did her friend who, though gone too soon, had done something outside the norm with her life. But worse, as certain as she was that Ida had gone into heaven to sit with the Savior, she knew that she herself would spend eternity in hell.

Betsy knelt when the minister called them to kneel. She recited by rote the passages of the service as they were spoken, grateful for the automatic motions. Her face was calm, stoic, and rock solid, a fact that Edmund noted. He also knew Betsy was a master at appearing strong when she was at her weakest.

When the service ended, she bundled the boys under the blankets, and they snuggled close to each other on the back of the sled. Edmund clicked his tongue, and the mare started forward, the bells on her harness ringing in the night. The tickle was frozen solid—this winter was colder than any they had experienced in recent memory. It had been solid for weeks now. He directed the animal to the place where they would cross to the southern island and the Elliott house.

The moon cut a wedge in the sky, and the stars twinkled a great distance away. The cold was biting, and the only visible parts of either adult were their eyes.

"I don't know how people handle such a loss," Edmund said when they were across the frozen tickle and headed home.

"Ida had a good and happy life. You think about that more than you think about the fact that they're gone."

"I suppose, but it seems so sad. A life cut so short. What's the point of it all, Betsy, to have so much to give and not be provided the opportunity to give it?"

"I thinks about it, and heaven knows I don't know. Maybe there's no point at all to it. I mean, the cemetery is jammed full of people, and nobody knows or remembers half of them, so what was the point? Work hard, build stuff up, slave to survive, only to die. It all rots around you while your bones rot in the grave, into the dirt."

"I guess we're supposed to just do what we can while we're here, live the best we can," Edmund said.

"My father used to say that we should set our sights on something bigger than we can ever imagine. He said each moment we live now determines a moment in our future. Each decision—and you makes hundreds in the run of a day—changes the course of your life. And the decision to do nothing changes it most of all."

"Your father sounds very wise."

"He was, though I don't suppose I know exactly what he meant by it. For me, I know what I'd like to do. I can see it in my mind. But I can't see how deciding to use white water to wash me apron over red water, or whether to use tinned milk over fresh from the cow, would get me any closer to it."

"What do you see, in your mind?" Edmund pulled the reins and slowed the horse, extending the drive home.

"I see leaving here, making my way, standing apart from the crowd. I always thought I'd do something, be something. I don't know why. I just grew up like every other girl. Worse off. But something, perhaps Father with his words about life and choices, made me think that I could do more. Perhaps it would have been better if he just hadn't filled my head with it all and left me to know this was all I could ever be."

"Betsy, if who you are right now is all you'll ever be, it's still more than most." Embarrassed by his words, Edmund snapped the reins, and the horse picked up speed.

"'Tis not enough for me, Edmund, but 'tis the best I can do."

They didn't speak for the rest of the journey. The night was silent except for the jingle of the mare's sleigh bells as they made their way to Elliott's Cove.

While Edmund settled the horse in the barn, Betsy fed the boys bread and molasses and weak tea with milk. They clung to each other under the weight of the quilts she had piled and among the heated rocks she had stuck beneath their feet to help stave of the night air that came through the wood-framed house like a frigid ghost. The heat from the brick chimney that backed onto the boys' room from the parlour helped keep the room above freezing, and Betsy decided she would sleep there and keep the fire going as the temperature plummeted by the hour. A check on John as she gathered her nightclothes worried her. He didn't respond to her questions, and her heart fluttered at the possibility that he was down for the winter.

In the kitchen, the big stove was hungry. Flames lapped at the quartered wood junks that Betsy shoved in there. She moved the pail of snow, then took a second bucket to get more to top it up. They had to melt snow for the horse as well as for themselves, and it was a constant chore. Edmund returned, and with barely a word, they handed off the pails. He gave her the one he had filled with snow and took the water for the horse.

In the barn, he petted and talked to Star with a soothing voice, loving how her coat grew thick in the cold of the winter. He brushed some snow off her and dried her legs with a blanket, then draped another blanket over her. It was unnecessary, as she was of hardy stock, but it seemed the caring thing to do. He stopped for a moment and rubbed the white mark between her intelligent, soft brown eyes, and she nudged his hand to show she liked it. Satisfied she was settled and safe, he left her and latched the door behind him.

The cold wind blew snow into drifts that needed to be shovelled away from the woodpile. Betsy heaved it over her shoulders as Edmund pulled junks free. The wind chopped at their faces and stung their lips. Betsy finished her chores before Edmund. Once inside, she put a kettle on for tea and checked on John once more. He still lay there, awake and unmoving. The recent news had caused this turn, she knew.

Knitting and sewing were not appropriate activities on Sundays, so she read.

"Any news?" Edmund asked, shaking the snow from his jacket and hanging it on the peg by the door. He shivered, his hands numb from the cold. The work he had done would have taken half the time, but with John sick and this cold snap, he was freezing. He handed Betsy the pail, which was filled again with snow. She stood and took it from him, noticing his raw hands.

"Are your feet like that, too?"

Edmund's teeth chattered. "They're frozen solid, Betsy."

"Get in the parlour. The fireplace is going, and it's nice and warm. There are blankets in there, and I'll bring water. Go."

"I need clothes. This is going to be soaked." The snow that clung to his clothes was melting in the heated kitchen, and his garnsey and shirt were getting damp.

"I'll get some. Get out of those wet clothes and into the blankets."

Betsy shivered as she entered his room to fetch some dry clothing. She set the lamp down and found a couple of items in his drawer, picking out nightwear that would be comfortable for him. She would encourage him to sleep in the parlour tonight to stave off a chill.

Downstairs again, she shut the door behind her and handed Edmund a nightshirt and long-legged underwear. She busied herself at the fire as he changed. The amber brass of the large mantel clock caught her eye, and in its reflection she saw him stand, drop the quilt, and begin to dress.

Edmund's legs were muscled from recent work. His flat stomach had a spattering of dark hair that sprinkled down from his chest. The glimpse of his expansive shoulders imprinted on Betsy the difference between the body of a young man and that of her husband, who was nearing fifty. In the brass, Edmund appeared golden, like the native man her grandmother Crane had told her she'd befriended as a young woman. Then the nightshirt fell over him, and she turned around.

The illusion evaporated. Edmund, pale as dust, shivered with lips still blue, and he shook his hands to bring the circulation back. Snapped out from her reverie, Betsy's natural inclination to dole out orders and take care of what needed caring for returned.

John had taken to his bed, and Betsy worried it was another bout of his sadness. And now here was Edmund on the brink of certain pneumonia. She wouldn't be saddled with two sick men if she could help it.

Edmund shivered under her ministrations as she pushed his bare feet into a pan of cold water to ease the chilblains that were the precursor of full-on frostbite. He flinched at the shock as it cooled the rest of him, something Betsy remedied by easing him back on the beaded cushion that decorated the settee as she tucked the blankets firmly around his neck. Twice now he'd almost frozen to death in this place, and twice Betsy had warmed him up.

"Thank you," he said, his voice more Bostonian than it had been since he had first arrived, and Betsy sat beside him and pulled a cold hand into hers and began to rub his fingers. When she felt that his right hand was good, she brought the left into her lap, and while she worked on it, Edmund drifted into a sleep that lasted even as she dried his feet. She put warm knitted vamps on them and tucked them under the covers. Afterwards, she tidied up the parlour and then the kitchen, returning once more to bank up the fireplace.

Before leaving, she knelt in front of Edmund in the dimly lit room to see how he looked. She touched his forehead and noted no fever and the return of some colour to his face. As she made to rise, his hand reached out and touched her cheek. Her brown eyes met his blue ones just before their lips touched.

Moments later, he lifted the blanket, and she slipped underneath it, as though it were all a big plan. There on the settee, underneath the quilt that had been hand-sewn by her mother-in-law, she gave into the gentleness and want that presented itself. He gave in, too, against his better judgment.

Edmund figured that since he was the next best thing to a murderer, the sins after that were not worth acknowledging, and as far as he could tell, a soul doomed to hell had no reason to avoid the pleasures offered on this earth, anyway.

TWENTY-SIX

On January 25, 1934, the sun moved upward in the eastern sky, creating a golden glow that lit the kitchen. Betsy pinned up her hair and secured it under a scarf tied at the back of her neck. She moved from the stove to the wash basin to clean the boys' faces, then sent them into the parlour while she readied their food.

Edmund walked into the kitchen, but she didn't look at him. She slipped a plate of food onto the table at his spot, then moved to lift a tray she had readied to take in to John, when her husband walked in and sat at in his place at the head of the table.

"You're up?" Betsy's eyes widened, and her mouth dropped open. She quickly composed herself and put the tray back, lifting the plate of warm food to set in front of John.

Edmund's belt felt tight around his waist, and his hand shook when he picked up his fork. He watched Betsy and knew that John's appearance had shocked her. She had expected him to be gone to bed for the winter, and that had been part of the motivation for her actions these past few nights. Now guilt sprang forth inside her, and her hands shook.

"You're feeling better, John?" Edmund broke the silence that was punctuated only by the distant ticking of the parlour clock.

"Was a bit of a fever, b'y," John answered. "Perfect now."

Betsy's eyes bored holes into John. She hadn't checked for fever, so sure was she in his taking to the bed for the winter that she had neglected to look for any other cause for his lie-in. In the past, he had always said he was sick, and she figured it was the same this time. She had delivered his food and he never spoke. But perhaps he'd slept? No. She didn't believe it. Maybe it was just a short spell, but surely it had been one of his fits.

The boys came tumbling into the room from the warm parlour, and John scooped up Richard.

"I figured the boys might be best away from me." John ruffled George's hair and set Richard on the barrel chair next to him. They reached for the food with their hands, then remembered, stopped, and picked up the forks their mother had taught them to use. Impulse was easily tempered by control and example, and she showed plenty of each.

Betsy got up to get the kettle for the tea right after saying grace. In her fluster over John's surprise recovery, she had forgotten to put it on. The wave hit as she poured water into the china pot to brew. She reached to steady herself. Her hand banged off the hot stove, striking the empty kettle, which clanged on its surface like a demented spinning top before Edmund grabbed its handle. A black hole beckoned her into it. John jumped to his feet and caught Betsy before she hit the floor.

The boys watched, eyes big like saucers, as the two men lowered their mother.

"What's happened to our mother?" George asked.

"I think she's got the fever, too," John answered, but when he touched her face, it was ice cold. A wave of terror spread over him. He flashed to the face of his first wife and her cold, dark complexion in a narrow wooden box, her skin taut like hide in the stillness of death. He had sought to lessen the likelihood of that in this strong and younger woman, and he feared to the depths of his soul he had failed.

"Edmund, go get Old Julie, now!"

But Edmund disobeyed. "Let's get her to the parlour first," he said, and before John could protest, Edmund tucked his arms under Betsy and lifted her.

He carried her into the warm room and set her on the same settee where they had been together the past few nights. She didn't stir. The task at hand distracted John from getting upset over the young man usurping his role by playing hero to his wife. He sat by Betsy and talked to her, encouraging her to wake up while Edmund fetched Old Julie.

Edmund cursed at the wind in his face but made his way to the stabled mare, harnessed her, and hitched her to the sled. He passed Walter John Parsons on the way and gave him a brief rundown of the events, at which point Walter John turned his pony around, the thought of cutting wood displaced by another thought as he headed back home.

Betsy did not regain consciousness until after Mrs. Parsons's serving girl came to the house. The young woman, delivered to their door by Walter John, jumped in to help. They were close neighbours, just two coves over, and he knew they would get there before Old Julie, who lived way down in Barrel Cove.

With consciousness came the same waves that had washed over Betsy, leaving her sweating under the blankets piled upon her. She sent John away with the boys, which he protested but was relieved about. He had no nerve for a sickroom, and the serving girl was as forceful as his own wife.

Kettles of water boiled on the stove when Edmund came in with Old Julie. She instructed him to bring more snow to melt.

"'Tis the youngster she carries, Julie," the young serving girl informed the midwife. "I can't feel it move, and I don't think it's moved for a long time."

Julie established that there was no fever and agreed that the flashes of heat were an indication that something had gone wrong inside Betsy's womb. She felt the bulge of Betsy's abdomen and noted that it was much too small for the time that had passed. She felt a hardening under her hand, and Betsy moaned under her breath.

"Is it feeling like you've taken sick, then?" she asked her patient.

Betsy nodded.

"We'll get you in the bed."

Edmund assisted as they got Betsy into her own bedroom. The midwife busied herself laying sheets under the bottom half of the bed, hoping it didn't take too long or cause too much trouble.

The warm rushes were soon accompanied by a familiar painful pattern, but unlike Betsy's previous births, this time she was too weak to work through them. She rolled in her bed, miserable from the strange, hot sensations that crept over her body each time a pain hit her. She drank steeped Labrador tea. It increased the pains, and she allowed herself some audible moans as she felt the tiny child move down though her body.

The young serving girl kept the water hot, moving in and out of the room. She took instructions from Old Julie, who delivered them in a kindly manner. The maid had a way of demanding respect, partly because of her abilities, and also because she carried herself like a woman far wiser than her years.

When the small, dead baby slipped from Betsy's body, it was Old Julie who wrapped the tiny girl in a white blanket and did a quick baptism. A child born dead wouldn't be baptized by a minister, but she performed the rite, anyway. There would be no funeral for this little soul, but it deserved some reverence and a chance to move toward heaven, even if it was a long shot.

The wilted afterbirth followed, along with more blood than normal. Julie pressed herbs into her to staunch the flow, and she massaged hard on the womb to make it stop. Once it did, Julie looked with horror at the scarlet linens and hoped that the bleeding had ceased before too much blood had been lost. It was close. If she made it, Betsy would be weak for some time.

Later, Julie took some liver pills from her bag and handed them to John.

"Will she live?" John asked the question and feared the answer.

"John, it's bad. It's not for sure, but she's tough, and if anybody can, it's Betsy," Julie answered, her teacup at her lips.

"Was it something that caused it?" Edmund stirred his tea, an action that was unnecessary as he drank it black.

"Hard to say, b'y," Old Julie answered, "but that little babe was dead a few weeks, for sure. Perhaps 'twas a shock. Sometimes this is the way it goes with babies. As many dies as lives, from what I sees."

Sadness fell upon John, as though a great hand had drawn a shade down over him.

As many dies as lives.

This was not true for him, for including his stillborn daughter, he had now lost four youngsters, and only two survived. If he were to lose Betsy . . . well, it was too hard to think about. He bowed his head over his teacup, his broken heart abiding with his lost children, as if unable to understand that part of it needed to stay with those still living. The sickness was as much from his mind as it was his heart, but it was his heart that drained his mind of the ability to cope.

John went and put his coat and boots on, then left for the store loft, a tiny bundle in a blanket tucked under his coat. After some time, he harnessed the mare and headed to the north end.

His mother's headstone rose tall and white, a twin to his father's in the snowdrifts. He shovelled away to solid ground, then grunted as he chopped into its frozen surface. As the hole grew deeper, the turf softened. He sweated as the wind stung his weathered cheeks. But no child of his would lie alone, and he whispered into the frigid air, "Mother, watch her little soul."

He buried the tiny child in the handmade box and covered it over. The minister didn't bury babies born too soon. They were hardly thought to be human at all, but John wanted this baby, born without breath, to at least be with family.

HE HATH AWAKENED FROM THE DREAM OF LIFE. The quote from the poet Shelley was etched into the foundation that held the double stones. John nodded at it, knowing to the marrow of his bones what the poet meant. And believing, too, that he soon would awaken. He considered life far more a nightmare than a dream these days.

* * * * *

The memory of an unconscious man's body falling to his death struck Edmund, as well as Betsy's lack of remorse over the entire thing. He wondered if she was being punished with the loss of her first daughter, and perhaps her own life, because of their mortal sin—or if perhaps the guilt of it all had stopped the baby from finishing its growing.

Edmund's sins built a wall of despair around him as guilt piled up like bricks, stacked one on top of the other, its mortar the lies told to cover those sins. This place of majesty and beauty held a darkness that was far beyond what he was capable of handling. It was all too late for him. He had already sinned more than any man should, and leaving wouldn't fix it. But it might help put the entire episode behind him. He should have done so before, but he renewed his determination now. The minute he knew for sure that Betsy would live, he would leave.

TWENTY-SEVEN

The lace in the window came from England with John Elliott's grandmother, who had made the curtains and hung them. Now a third generation saw the sunlight through the timeless pattern that created a luminous picture of flowers and ropes on the wide planked floors. Betsy stared in their direction but didn't see them, her thoughts on the frustration of being confined to a bed when there was so much to do.

A knock on the door was followed by it opening a crack. The voice behind it asked permission to come in, and Betsy sat up straight and patted her hair. It was braided down on one side, not up in a severe bun as usual. She couldn't sleep on it that way.

"Sure, come on in."

He entered, blocking the sunlight for a moment.

"You're feeling better, Betsy?" Edmund had been getting reports that she was, but he figured it was only fitting to check on her, too.

"I'm alive, and Julie said she had her doubts I'd make it, so I shouldn't complain, but I'm tired of being in the bed. Other than that, I'm good." Betsy believed it an absolute weakness to be lying around sick, but even that morning when she had gotten herself off the feather bed to use the chamber pot, a dizziness had forced her back in under the covers, shaking. Whatever Old Julie had given her had stopped the bleeding, but not before she was drained.

"I don't know how John manages to go to bed for months." She shook her head.

"I know you said that before. Does he get some sort of influenza?"

"No, not sick like that, but he gets to going to bed when things gets hard."

"He just goes to bed?"

"It's, well, he goes a bit mad." Betsy glanced at the door and then heaved a big, fear-filled sigh. She felt protective of John, too. The town talked when John took to bed, and they knew he wasn't sick in the body.

"Oh, God." Edmund was taken aback. John seemed so stable.

"When he gets too sad in his heart and he can't handle it, he takes to bed." Betsy's lips formed a tight, firm line as though to block more words.

"Everybody needs a bit of rest."

"It's far beyond rest. He goes into another place. I thought he had barred himself away that day after Ida died. I figured he was down for the winter and I would have to do it all again. One spring I had to get the gear up and ready for the schooner on the off chance he did come to. It was a hard winter, and that was when the boys were babies. He got up in time, though, and took to the Labrador all right, but only because I got it ready for him. I always hope 'tis just a nap, but the naps are for the daybed. When he goes to bed, that's not the same thing at all."

"You thought he got sick because of poor Ida?"

"I did, yes. He's been all worked up about the government and the country, and that plagues on his mind. It's like the minute a bad thing happens, and he knows somebody it happened to, it's the last thing he can take, and he gives up. Like when Clyde Waugh died."

"But that's not directly in the family. He was just a stranger."

"I know, and so I hope this winter he gets through. I suppose it was just a fever he had, but the signs is there it's coming on."

"What signs?"

Betsy let her mind go over them. The main one was a lack of attention to her in the bedroom, though she couldn't say so to Edmund.

"The winter, I suppose, being so hard, Clyde Waugh's being found dead here, the sickness on the go and worrying about the boys, now this with Ida. And me. Losing the—"

"What's he worried about the boys for?" Edmund didn't want Betsy to have to think about her lost baby.

"You don't know about his first family?"

"John was married before, and his wife died of a fever."

"See, John met his first wife on a fishing trip to Labrador. His father went down every year. Well, one year he got in go with this girl from down there, and anyway, the next year when he went back, she had a baby. It was his, she said, and he never doubted her, but his father was savage. But that was the only time John didn't listen to his father, and he went and married her. But that old bastard, he said fine, but no Indian was coming to his house, and if John didn't come back home with him, he'd not pay him."

"That's a terrible thing. What did John do?"

"Well, far as I know, he and his wife decided John would come home in the fall with his father and leave her there. So that's what they did, for several years. After that they had two more youngsters."

"My God. His father wouldn't give in?"

"No, and he would make him feel bad about his poor old mother, too. But that woman would have loved to have them here, but she had no say. Anyway, his father was in charge and, well, you'd have to know him, but nobody dared not listen to old George Elliott, and with John so easygoing, he left her a bit of money each year and come back. Then the last year, when he got to Labrador, his family had died. They had just died, too. Wasn't even buried yet. Spanish influenza. That's why John's so afraid of fevers."

"That poor man."

"It all happened before I was here, but it must have been some sad for him, and that wasn't the first time he took sick. The war was hard on John, too. He wanted to go, but he was sick for real with a fever that left him too weak to get in the army. He got so bad he could hardly walk. He was also the only one able to care for the family. Mrs. Elliott told me he found it hardest when young Archie Porter died, just eighteen years old, at the Somme, Beaumont Hamel. So many of the young men come back odd, you know, never the same."

"He felt bad about not going?"

"Yes. John is the nicest man in the world. But his heart is too soft, my son. Too soft for his own good. He could take a hammer to the head and never make a cry, but another man's hurt he feels to his soul. His mother said one year he come home one day in June and laid on the bed and never got up until the fall. Over four months he never spoke or got up. He ate what was brought but never done another thing. His father didn't have much patience for it and bawled at him, but nobody could shake him out of it. He sailed to Labrador without him that year."

"But he came out of it after a while?"

"Yes. He goes into it again from different things. The winter after his family died, he come back and was fine until after Christmas. Then an old horse that he owned fell in the bog, and they couldn't get her out. They had to shoot her so that she wouldn't smother in the mud. His mother said he shot that horse and watched her sink. He come home and took off his boots and went to bed."

"That was the last time?"

"No, there was the year his father died. I was here by then. It was the year my mother died, too. His father died in late December, and he got through very good. But then one day in February, he just never got up. That time was when we sent him to the Waterford. A local man was going to St. John's, and he took John with him. He was in there all winter and spring. I hauled me guts out that year—wonder we didn't freeze. Just me and the old lady, and lucky we had the grub in aforehand, or we would have. Then one day we got a telegram he was coming home."

"He was better?" Edmund asked.

"Seemed he was. We knew he improved because he wrote us a few letters, but then he came home. He didn't take the schooner off to Labrador that spring until long after everybody else had gone."

"But he did go to Labrador?"

"Had to," said Betsy. "Wasn't a fish to be caught in these waters that year. It was a short season, but he did it. Scrounged up a small crew and took the gear he had, which wasn't much, and sailed off. Got enough to get us through that winter, and he's caught up a good bit since."

"Yet you married him?"

"People wonders at that. They thinks I got caught or something, but truth was we become close friends. The winters after that, he was bright and happy. We went to the Candlemas time together that first year. We danced a lot, and he was good. But then the government thing started, and this thing they calls a depression, and there was hardly any money."

"Has it happened since you were married?"

"Just the one time, and only for a month. I don't even know what set him off that time."

"You think he'll get sick again?"

"I don't know." Betsy's voice was grim.

"But you think he might?"

"I thinks this might be the kind of year that drives him to it, yeah."

They both started when the bedroom door opened, then sighed in unison as young Mary walked in.

"So, you'll not be going to evensong tomorrow?" Edmund asked Betsy. This conversation wasn't a concern of Mary's.

"No, Julie says no church yet."

"I'll have to take young Mary on the sled with me."

Mary's smile was brighter than the sun that shone through the thin panes of glass. She left with Edmund as Betsy sat staring out the window, wishing she could go to church, too. Not that she enjoyed it all that much, but it was far better than being in bed doing nothing. If John wasn't down now, he could be before the season ended, and she knew exactly what a hard winter it would be if that sickness in his heart took hold again. She didn't know if she, as strong as she was, could bear it. Even with Edmund there to help.

TWENTY-EIGHT

Betsy recovered over the next week. When Edmund stopped by her room one day, he found her sitting in a chair, fully dressed.

"Good, you can bring me to the parlour. Julie says I can get up but needs to be walked alongside."

Edmund crooked out an elbow and aided her into the warm room. She didn't feel the least bit woozy, but she held on to him, anyway. The embarrassment of passing out in front of him would be greater than that of taking his help.

"John gone off with the gun?"

"Yes. Walter John come over, and they're gone off for some black ducks."

"Nice feed for dinner, then." There was no doubt they would come back with some.

"Mary coming to cook it?" asked Edmund. "She's doing a fine job these days."

"She is learning, but I'll cook it the right way." Her voice didn't betray her annoyance at his compliment of her cousin.

"You sure?"

"I will," she snapped. She jammed a knitting needle into the stitch on her other needle, and the two began a rhythm as her hands worked on a sweater that bunched in her lap. Edmund pulled a chair up and sat before her.

His eyes grave, he said, "I'm leaving, Betsy. I have to go."

Click-click-click. The needles made a low scraping sound between each stitch as they were brought back and inserted again and again. Betsy's eyes never left them until she turned the work around and started the next row, interrupting the rhythm of her needles for only a moment.

"How?"

"It's froze solid now. I'll get into Lewisporte across the run, by horse, perhaps. I suppose I could go on the mail plane to Botwood, too. One or the other."

"When?"

"Soon as I get things arranged."

The clock on the mantel quietly repeated its tick-tock along with her needles, until eventually the two sounds blurred into one. As he waited in the quiet, Edmund could have sworn it was the clock that conformed to Betsy's rhythm and not the other way around.

"Why?"

"Betsy."

She looked at him in the dark crimson chair with its mahogany arms. He filled it up, as it was a lady's seat. Edmund looked down into her eyes, and she looked from them back to her knitting.

"Betsy, I can't stay here anymore." He had prayed more in the past few weeks than he had ever prayed before.

"Why can't you? Too rough for you? I suppose it's a hard life for a man not used to it." The dart went straight through his pride, and she knew it.

"Hard? My God, Betsy, young Mary was attacked and hurt . . . we killed a man." He said the latter in a low voice, then raised it again. "Then poor Ida's funeral, John got sick, you got sick. It's not hard, Betsy, it's impossible. And then we—that was wrong, Betsy. I wasn't raised to all this wrong."

"Wrong? You think I was raised to *wrong*? I was reared to *do*, Edmund. To survive. We done what the law wouldn't do. That girl would be ruined by that Clyde Waugh, and we women needs to take care of that stuff ourselves. You didn't have to touch him. You did, and fine, but grow up. This isn't the big city, where you gets to call the constable over every little thing. You saved all the women that man would have ever touched. As to you and me, what odds. What's done is done now. You want to leave, then leave. I never asked you here, anyway."

"Are you not afraid of going to hell, Betsy?"

"Hell? Hell is winter when you're stuck with an old lady and man took to his bed because it's too much trouble to get up. When spring comes and the cellar is low and the only thing to do is to take to the ice yourself to get a seal to eat, or perhaps a couple ducks. When you shuts the parlour down because the wood is low and nearly freezes all March month to make do. When you take your babies on a sled into the woods to cut enough to get through, and some man looks at you like you're a meal of seal yourself, and only the infant inside your coat stops him from havin' a go. When you piles up the sled and has to stop to give the baby milk because you had nobody to leave him with and you're worried your other baby will freeze before you gets home. Hell is when you goes into service at ten or when your mother puts your sisters on a steamer for the orphanage because your father died of the fever. I don't concern myself with hell. I figures I'm in it most winters, and a bit of heat from the brimstone would be welcome. If it is a choice between the frost and the fire, what would you pick?"

Edmund stepped back. Betsy's passion frightened him but intrigued him as well.

Click-click-click. Across she knit again, her hands moving the wool over the long needle, pulling it back through, *click*, again and again. He was mesmerized that these large, calloused hands of hers, so unlike the women of Boston, could be so deft and delicate and creative as a pattern emerged from the wool, twisted and roped into a cable.

"Leave, my son, go on and leave. We don't need you. John is good enough this winter, and the boys is bigger, and if he gets sick, what odds?"

Edmund remained silent as he leaned back in the chair. He looked around at the parlour. A needlepoint in a ring was on a shelf, the patterns emerging from the dark background. He had seen Betsy work on that on another day when the sun was bright through the windows. The rug on the floor was handmade, and he knew she had made it, too. There were monograms on their shirts now, as fine as any he had ever seen, and a new project awaited by the sewing machine. Her friend had brought her ten sewing needles for it, won through some sales contest in the *Twillingate Sun*. Betsy had helped deliver her baby, and the needles were a present for delivering him.

This house was full of Betsy. She was skilled at all she tried her hand at, and it didn't surprise him that she was as handy with a gun as she was with a needle. He knew nothing of sewing but felt that her work was superior. But it wasn't right. This life was so hard and the sins too many. He needed to get away from the place. *She* did, too.

"Then you come with me. You come along to Boston and get away from all of this."

The clicking needles stopped, and the clock ticked solo.

"Go with you? To Boston?" She laughed, but stopped when he didn't join her. "I've a life here, Edmund. I've two boys to take care of."

"They can come, too." He surprised himself again.

"What was in the tea, Edmund? You're as mad as John is, I think."

"Just come with me, and we'll tell them in Boston that you're a widow. Use your maiden name, give it to the boys. Nobody will know the difference."

"You means it, don't you? What about John?"

"Yes, Betsy, I mean it. Come to Boston with me." He ignored the question about John. That was for her to decide, but in the moment, he had asked her. He knew he wanted her to come with him, to bring the boys, and she would have a life away, a decent life for her and her sons with his support. The idea appealed to him, and he rose and looked down at her.

"I mean it. If this is so hard, then I'll take you and the two boys, and we'll go." He walked from the room, the offer made.

In all her life, Betsy had not seen that there was any likelihood she would go anywhere. This life was hell on earth at times, but it was all she knew. Leaving would kill John, especially if she took the boys. Or at least drive him into whatever world he liked to spend his time in when the madness hit. Her place was here, not off traipsing around Boston. Her boys were island boys, and if they grew up and wanted to go, they could go.

Boston. With trains and universities and opportunities and so many people. It was the city of her dreams, the place she was supposed to decide in this moment whether to take a step toward. She wanted it. It was all she had ever wanted.

Duty pinned her to the couch, knitting a sweater for her husband. It bound her to this land, where life was rough and starvation lurked around every hummock and over every shoal. When times were at their worst, the weather often dropped them into further despair, and when it seemed like a bit of a break was coming, the government would give them a smack in the face that made the northeast wind seem like a gentle breeze. But still, her roots were deep, past sea level, and her life was on this shore.

As the clock on the mantel ticked away, the sun broke through the dark sky—the weather here shifted with each tick of the timepiece. It peeked through the clouds that had held it in check these past ten minutes. The heat warmed Betsy's face, and her heart hammered in her chest. There was a new feeling in it. Something she hadn't felt since her father died and dreams became something she escaped to and not something that could come true. Now this *thing* was before her, and she didn't quite know what to do with it. She played with the offer in her mind, dismissed it as utter foolishness, then reconsidered once more. Duty said no, her heart yearned yes. For the first time in a long time, Betsy's dreams had a possibility of being realized.

It unsettled her more than the wind that blew through the cracks and made her shiver and pull her shawl closer. Her needles began to click again. The wind changed direction again, and she could smell the damp odour of the pots that boiled in the small store next to the house where the men picked the seabirds. She knew they would be in with them soon. She set the knitting aside and made her way to the kitchen, pleased that the dizziness had left her, and crediting the seal liver that Old Julie had brought her. She also credited the cod-liver oil she had forced herself to swallow. Betsy pulled open the stove and poked at the fire. She would get the youngsters back over from the Scammells' tomorrow. Ada and Millie had taken the boys, who loved playing with Millie's girl, Hazel. But it was time to bring them home. She liked having them around, and they would distract her from the silliness in her now. She could no more take the boys to Boston than she could fly to the moon.

"Go to Boston? Too foolish to talk about," she said to the empty kitchen. "'Tis too darned foolish to even talk about."

But Betsy wasn't all practicality and stoicism. If her father had put one thought in her head, it was that she was the maker of her own destiny, the walker of her own walk. The paths of possibility were two-fold, and in the end she had no idea which one she would take.

TWENTY-NINE

The full moon lifted itself above the frozen, barren sea. Dunes of snow overlapped like a desert of white sand. The powerful moon pulled against the earth below, and the tide heaved its mighty shoulders up underneath the ice. It swelled and rose and grumbled for space, confined by the heavy ceiling, wanting freedom. It pushed and groaned and eventually weakened the fissures where the floes had adhered to each other in the frigid air of the coldest winter seen in fifty years.

When the tide battled the cold, the tide won, and the ice began to break up from the island of Baccalieu, around the ballycater first, then all along the west side of the land and through the main tickle that ran between the two islands.

The release of the tide spread south to north, cracking a wide rent in the fabric of the white seascape. In a matter of twenty-four hours, it could no longer be traversed by horse or man out past the immediate shores. Oceangoing traffic was likewise impossible.

Isolation was now complete.

It didn't much matter to a self-sufficient community settled in for a winter with sod cellars full of turnip and potatoes. Bags of split peas, dried beans, and dried fish filled pantries and stores. Seals came near and were hunted, ducks were shot from behind gazes that had been built when the place was settled, and men were adept at copying the tightly woven ice pans to retrieve them with one eye to the wind and another to the shifting tides. It was hard. A few souls wouldn't make it through. That was the way of things.

February 17 dawned bright and cold. Candlemas Day, the holiday that celebrated the presentation of Jesus at the temple forty days after his birth, was a reason for a winter ball in this small place, but the weather had interfered, and so it was delayed, much to Betsy's delight. She had still been weak on February 2, but now she was fully recovered from her illness. The tickle had jammed up, and they could get across to the other side, though the wester' run was still all apart. While the hall was being set up for the dance, the lanterns and pot-bellied stoves were lit and the accordion players practised a jig with a bit of a swig for the events. Instead of helping, Edmund stayed home and readied himself in his room. He was trapped here, navigation effectively closed until later in the spring. He couldn't bother people to take him across the run just because he was uncomfortable. He would have to stick it out another while.

Edmund was warm. The heat from the fireplace was a constant now that Betsy had recovered. He realized he looked fancier than the other men, but he had no choice. These were the clothes he had. The men dressed in their Sunday good stuff, but none of it was as fine as the suit he wore from Felene's.

He never spoke of the fineness of the people he associated with in Boston to anyone but Betsy, who loved to hear him talk of it. He sometimes worried he sounded like he was bragging, but she insisted it didn't sound like that at all. She just wanted to know what it was like.

Katrina crossed his mind. He hadn't thought of his old girlfriend in ages. Her family was wealthy, and when they were together, Edmund had deferred to her on all matters of taste. When she accompanied him to the store to purchase new clothes, she mentioned in passing that the owner was a family friend. She had introduced him to Edward Felene. Edmund had been enthralled by the fellow and spent many hours reading his philosophies. They had influenced him a great deal. He always thought of her when he put on the suit she had helped him choose, but he couldn't picture her anymore. Her face had faded from his memory.

All thoughts of Boston, Felene's department store, and Katrina vanished when he walked into the parlour and caught sight of Betsy. She avoided his eyes as she readied herself for the "time," as they called it here. The Candlemas Ball was the dance of the year, and the women all dressed their very best. Betsy had an advantage. An annual catalogue, paid for by her mother-in-law, still came to the house. That shrewd woman had taken advantage of a multi-year price for her subscription, and from its pages the inspiration for her dress was found. Adding her own brilliant knack for creative design, Betsy had sewn something beautiful to wear.

Instead of making a dress out of the fabric John had given her for Christmas, she refurbished an old dress belonging to her mother-in-law. Betsy was a foot shorter and much smaller, so there was plenty of material. The royal blue was rich and one of the best dresses remaining in the trunk. A small jacket fashioned from a contrasting cream with a little ruffle around her hips, in the style of the catalogue photo, completed the look. The full skirt narrowed, but the flaring at the bottom left just enough leg room for a good dance.

Face scrubbed, lips pinched, nose powdered, and cheeks slapped to pink, Betsy was ready. She had twisted her hair atop her head with several pins and held it fast with a large hair comb. It was simple, save for three smart pearls. This was her mother's only bequeathal to her, and she had fastened a ribbon to it to add a further decoration that mimicked the hats of the day.

Edmund's admiration was obvious, and she felt the compliment before he spoke.

"You look beautiful, Betsy." The simple phrase was the first of many words of praise she would receive that evening yet would be the most treasured.

John came into the room, holding his hat in his hands, eyes distant, looking through Edmund and Betsy at some space on the wall.

"I'll go, I suppose, but I'm not up for dancing much. Perhaps, Betsy, you'll plank her down with Edmund a few times, because I know you loves a good stomp."

Betsy and Edmund locked gazes. Their superficial thoughts had fled with John's expression and his monotone words. Worry for John dampened their enthusiasm, but they carried on getting ready.

John came around a bit and was almost back to himself when they reached the Society of United Fishermen Hall. The bustle of friends gave him energy, and he hoisted himself up taller as he was acknowledged by the men who, while not quite understanding the weaknesses of the man, held him in high esteem.

THIRTY

Mary was a server, which was a clever way for a girl too young for the ball to take part in it. She worked the tables, and when the time came, she asked to be able to serve her family—John, Betsy, and Edmund, who sat next to his aunt and uncle. Her own parents were at home with the children, including George and Richard.

She weaved in and out as she served food to the attendees and made sure the water glasses and teacups remained topped up. Pipes that smelled of apples and cinnamon lit up as men leaned back on chairs and took in their surroundings once their stomachs had been filled.

By and by, tables were cleared and pulled back and chairs set to the middle of the hall by those who had attended this dance many times. Mary's eyes followed the action, watching as John shifted to sit near J. H. Scammell. His cousin, Art, who would normally sing or play some songs at a time like this, was off teaching this winter. It was too bad, because the crowd spoke of how they missed him.

Many considered young Scammell to be a bit conceited or, as they phrased it, big in himself, for going off to college in St. John's and getting all fancy. Some in the crowd were quite brutal in their verbal attacks on him. It was pure jealousy. When he wasn't there, they lamented that they wouldn't get to hear him sing that good song he always sung about the squid jiggin'. Skipper John Chaffey was always interested in hearing it, perhaps because his name was in it, but mostly because it cut down the townies and made fun of their silk hankies. There was nothing worse than a fancy townie to the crowd here. The ones who got all grand by going away weren't as bad as those who came from there to start with, but almost.

When Edmund was a boy and said he was going away to Boston, a group of kids had beaten him up for daring to state such a stupid thing, calling him big in himself and a liar. But he hadn't been lying. The Taylors—his mother's people, who had relocated to Boston—had promised his grandmother that Edmund would be educated at Harvard and had arranged the money for his tuition. He had grown up with the expectation, and when it was shown that he had the aptitude for it, his mother had made it her duty to ensure it happened. His father's death had been a tragedy in his young life, but it gave his mother the freedom to go back home to her family.

Outside the circle of John Elliott's friends, Edmund endured stares of resentment and felt the threat of those same bullies who had jammed his face into the ice, leaving a good drop of his blood pooling and freezing on the path home from the Church of England school.

They still noticed *him*, too. Furthermore, they saw how every single female and a few married women turned their heads in Edmund's direction when he came into the lodge. Several set their sights on the young man, and there was a constant traffic of females who "must have a word with Betsy about her dress" more than ever before.

Betsy saw through their intentions when their eyes rested on Edmund as they paid their compliments.

John perked up when he realized there might be a bit of sport here. "Sure, the maids are thick, b'y, for a fellow like you." He elbowed the young man and pulled on his pipe, exhaling apple-scented smoke.

"Lots of lovely ladies, yes." Edmund agreed with a nod and watched as Ada Scammell walked by with her mother, Althea, her eyes bright and her smile quick, and her friend who walked with them gave her a subtle elbow as if to acknowledge him as a potential mate.

Betsy's eyes flashed as she saw Edmund watching Ada. Her dark hair and skin were in stark contrast to her lovely off-white dress. Betsy had sewn lace over the shoulders of her homemade dress. She had made it herself with a fine thread unravelled from some old dresser covers she had found in the attic. Her dress was as fine as Ada's, yet she knew that Ada's had been ordered in, and she also knew that everybody else knew. It rankled her. But she had no idea that Edmund was comparing the two women in his mind and thinking that Betsy's dress appeared to be much finer than Ada's and was calculating that the dress she wore would be in great demand and would fetch a good penny in Boston.

John's spirits didn't pick up enough for him to join in the dancing, and when the night started with the Change Islands reel, Betsy's favourite dance, he motioned for his wife and Edmund to take to the floor without him. The accordion started with a great chord, launching into the tune with gusto. Another player waited nearby, toes tapping, instrument at the ready for when the first became too tired to carry on. There were three in all, their eyes bright and smiles quick with anticipation.

It started off sensible enough. A few novice dancers learning the moves were accounted for, and their mistakes made for the best of the fun. A perfect reel was never danced, and the willingness of somebody new to take a chance was always the best part.

Betsy was no novice, and in her newly sewn dress with just enough give that she could race in and around and under arms, stomping her feet as the tempo increased, sitting, being tossed, being swung, her eyes glowed as bright as a cat's in the flickering light of the lanterns. Edmund danced a bit too much like a gentleman but kept up all the same with the boisterous arm-tossing and swinging of the others. His reservation melted, and he lost himself in the wildness of it all as the laughter burst from Betsy the way the water bubbled out of the brook from where she brought the water. Her feet were light, and she flew freely around and through the pattern of the reel, spinning, ducking under that arm and this one, and always when they touched she smiled straight at him, until her eyes were all he could see, no matter who held his hand.

Nobody noticed when they switched accordion players except those who knew music so well that it was as if a different voice had spoken up. Betsy was one of those, having picked up many instruments by ear, and she gave a huge smile at the switch that Edmund hadn't noticed at all. He was so lost in the dance, so entranced by the woman he danced with, that he didn't notice much of anything.

After it ended and before the next dance began, the laughing couple returned to their table, and Betsy drank a glass of cold water. Her skin glistened in the amber light, and her long eyelashes curled up over the roundness of her eyes. Her cheeks flushed, and her lips shone from the water. All signs of the brusque, no-nonsense woman had vanished along with the cares she bore most days.

Despite her serious qualities—her strength, her work ethic, her sense of duty—Betsy knew how to have a bit of fun when the time was right. Edmund made the surprising realization that this was what he loved most about her.

THIRTY-ONE

She came into John's room that night without a sound. He was already under the covers in the dark. At first he thought it was a dream because he didn't hear the door open and close. No candle or lantern was lit, but he could see the outline of her face. Her eyes crinkled at the corners, and she smiled and came over to the bed and stood above him.

He didn't reach for her and didn't think anything much of it when the room got brighter and she was clear in his vision.

She hadn't been to see him in a long time, and he had missed her.

"How are the youngsters?" he asked.

She stood for a moment and then perched on the bed. He felt her weight tugging the patchwork quilt tight over his body and knew that she was real.

"They are happy and well," she replied, reaching up to stroke his forehead. She brought her hand down over his cheek as though to wipe away the lines and wrinkles that had settled into it since she had last touched his face.

"I am sorry I left." He apologized again as he had apologized to the air and the wind and the parson who had held him when he had been a distraught man on that cold Labrador evening when he had returned to a dead family.

"It was what had to be done." Mere's voice had not changed. Time had not worked its perils on it. It did not crack as his did with the passing of the seasons that tightened his joints and weathered his skin.

She wore the dress she had worn when he had embraced her and promised to return for her and bring her home with him next fall. His father was ill and would not live the winter, and it was he who had refused to allow John to bring his bride. His mother was gentle and would allow her and her grandchildren to be part of their home. After all, there were Labrador brides all over Notre Dame Bay, even if his father thought one wasn't good enough for his son.

The last time she appeared, John waited for her in the room, lying still, ignoring the world until she came to him. She sometimes brought their children, and he would watch as they played on the floor, the little girl as pretty as one of those girls in the Sunlight soap ads. The little boy was very much like himself and the baby at her breast dark like his mother and grandfather, with a shock of ebony hair. He could see his looks in the oldest children. The baby didn't appear to have any white, but he knew it was his son.

There was not much time together, but enough to make babies and enough time to get married.

The same pride that had made his father refuse to have a Labrador native live in their house as a daughter-in-law made the son refuse to have bastard children. He loved her in a way that frightened him, and when she died, after working as hard as any man on the coast that season of fishing, he returned home to mourn.

That was the first time she had visited, and it wasn't until Mere stopped coming by each night that he got out of bed again.

He reached out for her hand, and she pulled away before he could touch it. She rose from the bed and walked toward the window.

"Carry on, John. You've work to do. But I'll be back in a few weeks. Then I'll stay."

"You will? I'll be here. I'll be ready," he said to her as she walked away and disappeared.

* * * * *

The hallucination, the spectre, the mystery of what he saw, lingered the next morning. Betsy was already up, so he remained in bed for a while, the night leaving him slowly. He would get up. He would do all that needed to be done until her return.

That February 18 morning saw a new spring in his step and life in his bones. Surprised that Betsy wasn't in the kitchen, he banked up the stove and put a kettle on, whistling as he did so. He slipped into his jacket and hat and put on a pair of trigger mitts. He glanced around, thinking it strange that she hadn't started tea. He grabbed the gun off the rack.

Betsy let out a squeal when she saw it and John's grim face as he stared down the barrel at the floor.

"Oh. Sorry, Betsy. I was just off to see about a couple of ducks. I knows 'tis Sunday, but I figured might be a good few around off the head since the water opened up."

Betsy nodded as he tucked the gun under his arm, the stock behind him on a forty-five-degree angle, and left. After the door shut, Edmund slipped into the kitchen behind her.

"What's he doing with the gun?"

"Goin' for a duck, he says."

"Oh, good. I thought he was going for me," Edmund said, only half joking. He spun Betsy around, and she dropped the curled chovies on the floor as he kissed her on the lips.

He pulled her skirt up, crumpling it bit by bit, his eyes on John's retreating back through the windowpanes. Betsy sighed and opened for him as his hands touched her bare skin. A quick tug at the front of his pants, and he was ready.

A while later, they heard the shotgun and giggled at its timing.

"I love you, Betsy."

Betsy smiled behind his ear as her skirt fell back down.

It vanished a moment later when the gun fired a second time. Two ducks were all they needed for supper, and John hadn't walked far. And Mary would be back from fetching the boys from her mother's place soon. She scooted away with a grin, her heart beating fast with the excitement and wrongness of it all.

The kitchen warmed under Betsy's firm hand on the poker. The kettle boiled as the fat in the frying pan sizzled for the morning meal. Edmund headed to his cold room to change out of his dancing clothes and to give the appearance of just getting up, when John returned. Edmund had spent the night in the parlour with Betsy, where he had woken on an empty settee with a dead fireplace, chilled to the bone and guilty as sin.

Betsy sang under her breath, the little jig that ended the dance the previous night looping around in her brain. John came in for breakfast a while later. She hoisted the big pot onto the stove and filled it with water from the barrel.

"I'm going to pick the birds in the back room, Betsy. Not up for lighting the stove in the store."

"It's Sunday, John."

Betsy didn't approve, but her mood was better than usual, and she left John alone about it. The song was still on her lips as Edmund entered the kitchen for breakfast, and he was more than pleased because he knew that he was the one who had put it there.

THIRTY-TWO

The cold gnawed like a wounded animal. The town huddled in, the woods too harsh now for anyone to cut wood. The radio and newspaper described the coldest winter on record across the country, and reports out of the United States and Canada were the same. In fact, the prairies of Canada and the states down through western America recently endured a drought and now suffered a great deal. The depression raged on, and the effects of the economic collapse were felt in the farthest corners of North America.

Fish prices had been at their lowest in years, and though fishermen with stores in their cellars and pantries might not starve, it would be hard to make do. The bays were frozen, preventing the hunters from getting out in their boats to get ducks, and the floes had not brought the nourishing seals close by. Desperation fell like a curtain on the most vulnerable. Houses with two or more fishermen could sustain their families but had none to share with neighbours who felt the sting of hunger as they spared their provisions. Children grew thin. Their eyes, sunken in their faces, looked large, wounded, and hungry. Babies were lucky to live their first year, and those who did often fell victim to one of the diseases that would run rampant through a body already tortured by malnourishment.

Rickets deformed young bones and stunted the growth of many who survived. Fevers weakened others over the long, cold winter months.

Betsy kept her sons from all social interaction. She refused to take them to church when bad diseases like diphtheria were reported. The stories of the epidemic of the 1890s were still fresh, the horror of it passed down through the generations. Scarlet fever, consumption, and influenza threatened them all, and children were especially susceptible. Betsy always read the health reports in the *Twillingate Sun* and heeded the warnings that spoke of communicable diseases and their prevention. Her pantry was well-stocked with jams and preservatives she had learned to create from her mother. Many of the island woman had no idea how to make preserves in jars. She had shown her closest friends, like Mervina, but others outside her immediate circle might not know how. Her grandmother had been a member of the Women's Institute in England, and she often lamented that Newfoundland needed such an organization to go from community to community, teaching skills such as the preservation of berries in jars.

But the women of the island were skeptical of the process, and even when they weren't, they could hardly afford jars for the berries. Betsy was lucky. When she had moved in with the Elliotts, as poor as she was, Fanny Crane had one thing of value. She brought her mother's remaining canning jars, and the Elliott family had been delighted with the results of her preservatives. They, being so well-off, had ordered more jars for the process. Betsy carried on that tradition, making jams and jellies and jarring anything requiring preservation for a cold winter.

John worked harder than he had in any winter gone by, and the woodpile was stacked high and the store brimming with activity. The mending of canvas and nets went on into the evening.

It thrilled Betsy to see her husband so well. As much as she thought of Edmund's offer to take her away to a whole new life, she wanted John well if she were to go. He was her duty, and she was beholden to her commitments. If she decided to go, she would only do so if he were well. Who would take care of him should she leave and he was sick?

Though he worked, he was not quite right. John was not preoccupied with the events unfolding in St. John's, and that was strange. His passion for the country had vanished, while it was Edmund and Betsy who huddled in front of the radio and over the *Twillingate Sun* for every peck of news. They discussed the commissioners who were chosen and the choices they might make for the country in these most desperate times. But John never came up from the store loft, choosing instead to eat and go back out to work.

It was unusual for him, but it was good because he was industrious, and that indicated strength to Betsy. The days rolled over, and Betsy marked them off on a calendar from Andrew Bown's store that had a picture of a pretty girl with brown hair. She kept a journal of the weather and noted daily events in a sentence or two like her mother had before her. It was an endless winter that saw more breath and death than most. She birthed babies with Old Julie, and only two had died since Christmas, making it a good year. March approached, and that's when things usually got worse.

John's strength gave hope to Betsy. In some ways the lure of a different life was easier to resist if she knew she wouldn't be facing life here alone. On the other hand, if John got sick, she knew she'd stay by his side, as her vows demanded. She didn't know what to do, so she didn't think of it except during rare moments when the walls closed in and the night fell about her after another day of not doing one single thing differently than she had done the day before.

THIRTY-THREE

John's hands ached. His back was sore, and his feet were blistered. But he carried on, propelled forward by a promise. He didn't dream of Mere, he didn't see the apparition that had told him that she would return, but there was a belief deep in his soul that she was real, so he worked hard to make sure that he was prepared.

The days were as long as the month of February was short, and he filled them with work. He didn't once consider what she meant when she had said she would return—or what would happen when she did. His delusion was such that it didn't matter. All he felt was a desperate need to be ready for it. He leaned back on the daybed in the kitchen and closed his eyes. Life happened around him, and he acknowledged it only on the surface, but he was not in it. Living, for John, was now something to do until his new life began again with Mere.

Mary came to the house every day to help Betsy in any way she could, reassuring her that she didn't need to be paid for every minute. The girl simply wanted to be with Betsy and learn her skills. Betsy was having the easiest February of her life in the sense that she had two extra hands around, one helping John and one helping her. Mary kept Betsy's bed free of children, too, who cuddled with this girl they adored in a big feather mattress.

For Betsy, it was a pleasant if confusing time. Helping Mary with some extra studies so she could be a teacher stimulated Betsy's quick mind, adding a new element to her day, and the little boys were starting to get older and more capable of caring for themselves. She felt compelled to help Mary because she enjoyed it, but she also realized how the Mondays she spent helping her had made her school success more challenging than it needed to be. Betsy hadn't considered it, as she had not gone past grade nine herself. And though Mary's family needed the money, and Mary had thrived despite so many days off, Betsy was determined to make this time easier for her cousin.

John ignored her at night, and she was grateful, especially when it was her time of the month. She was concerned that her messing around with Edmund would leave her with a souvenir that she wouldn't be able to explain to her husband, who hadn't touched her in a long while.

Edmund had finished much of his written work and was now revising his paper, a job he sometimes did in the kitchen after the evening cleanup when the boys were tucked away, the news finished, and the radio shut down. February 27 found him sitting and reading by lantern light as he shuffled through papers, scratching out this thing, rewriting that. Nearby, in the kitchen, Betsy worked on a rug in the rocking chair while John lazed on the daybed and Mary looked through a catalogue. When Edmund closed his book and leaned back in his chair, Mary made to speak but was cut off by Betsy.

"You're all finished? Put the kettle on, Mary."

Edmund looked at Betsy with admiration in his eyes, and it irked Mary. She was glad Betsy was married. Mary felt she was pretty and smart enough to be a good wife. She ignored the local talk of a girl in

Boston who waited for Edmund. It was likely gossip, and as she had told Ada Scammell, just because a girl waited didn't mean the man was going to show up.

"Yes, finished for now." Edmund picked up his papers and headed to the bedroom. John, hearing the movement from the daybed, rose and announced that he would go to bed as well.

"Would you like a cup of tea, Betsy?" Mary had recently determined that she must speak better, and her offer sounded formal. And now that she had Betsy alone, she had exciting news to tell her.

"Yes, maid, that's why I said put the kettle on." Betsy pulled over the catalogue that Mary had abandoned and flipped through it.

Mary stoked the fire, placed the kettle on the stove, and grabbed a tin of sweets she'd baked. It irritated Betsy that they were so good. Or perhaps she had been irritated by how Edmund had raved about them when the girl had offered him one after supper. Betsy shook off her jealousy and opened the lid when Mary handed her the tin. After all, she, not Mary, had been invited to run away with Edmund. Mary was a lovely young girl, and she would make a fine teacher.

Mary hesitated, then forged ahead.

"Betsy, you know how I said I wants to be a teacher before I gets married."

"Well, my dear, you'll have to quit the first when you do the second, you know that, right?"

"Yes, but I want a family sometime. I don't want to stay here forever, either."

"It's a hard life here, for sure, my dear."

"You ever want to leave?"

"No."

"Never?"

She watched Mary bring the teapot over and set it on the table. It would be black tonight with no sugar. Betsy had decided to cut it out for Lent and only indulge on Sundays.

"I never want to leave," Betsy said, knowing it was a bald-faced lie. In summer when she slaved from dawn till midnight, in harsh winters when John was sick, in moments when the world closed around her and the days melted into each other with drudgery, Betsy wanted to flee from this place. Edmund's offer of a different life was something she had considered and rejected every single day since it had been made. She had finally admitted to herself that she was undecided, but she couldn't risk even a hint of that to this girl.

"I never want to leave, and I'm never going to leave."

Mary smiled. "Do you think, now that I finished up my exams, Edmund will take me back to Boston?"

Betsy felt her lip burn. She blew on the tea. "That's a lot to ask, Mary, maid," she said simply, hiding her shock.

"Well, I know that, but I was thinking that instead of teaching I could go into nursing. Boston has a good school."

"Money is the problem."

"I have it."

"What do you mean, you have it? Where did you get that kind of money?"

"I visited Mrs. Parsons and asked her. I said I wanted to be like Ida and have a life. I said I wasn't sure I wanted to be a teacher or a nurse, but I think a nurse would suit me best, and I needed money for that. I asked for a loan and said I would pay her back, and she said yes!"

"You did what?" Betsy stood, seething. "You went begging to poor Mrs. Parsons?"

"It wasn't begging—"

"We don't ask for money from people. That's not our way. What must she think? Why didn't you ask us? She must think we're on the dole or something." Betsy pushed her chair back and slapped her hands on the table.

Mary jumped, and her eyes watered. "But I needed the money." Her own family had been the recipient of so much charity, she had no idea there were people who would feel shame at the idea.

But the Elliotts were a proud bunch, and Betsy was proud to be one of them. She wondered how many people knew that her cousin had gone to the Parsons family for money instead of the Elliotts and what they would make of that.

"How much do you need?"

Mary whispered the amount, and Betsy was floored. Mary kept talking. She had it all worked out and had already written the school. The young girl had discussed her plans with her teacher, who had encouraged her and written a recommendation.

"I will lend it to you."

Betsy had no right to make the offer without John's approval, but she did, anyway. She was thrifty and had stashed quite a bit of money away, a bit more than Mary needed. It was her insurance against John's illness, her travel money if she decided to leave. She had hidden it in a tin under some old blankets in the old wooden wardrobe in her bedroom.

"You have it?"

Mary was surprised. She had heard Betsy's lamenting, had heard the stories about how their incomes had gone down, how the low price of fish had made this a hard year for them as it had for everyone. Even the Parsonses, who were better-off than most, had suffered.

Betsy sighed in defeat. "Yes, I do. So, tell Mrs. Parsons that you'll be borrowing from your own family if you gets into nursing school."

"You think Edmund will take me?"

"That, my love, is something to ask Edmund."

THIRTY-FOUR

"So, you said yes to her?"

Mary had been full of excitement when she informed Betsy that she was indeed going to Boston. All sorts of letters were being written by her teacher and her parents, the minister, and others to get Mary into the nursing school, and Edmund's endorsement would seal the deal. She would live with his family while she attended. They were charitable toward people from their old home island and had plenty of space to accommodate the young woman, whose life would be changed by their kindness.

"I didn't know how to say no, Betsy," Edmund answered. His voice was low and conspiratorial, though the house was empty. "I mean, 'tis a chance for Mary to do good, to be somebody. Her mother and father agreed. Though they said they'd never let her travel alone to Boston, they allowed that she could come with me."

They saw a future son-in-law in Edmund and had of course agreed. They were more interested in marrying her off than her having a career, and Betsy wasn't sure that Mary wasn't thinking along the same lines. She didn't know if she should tell Edmund her suspicions or if he would accuse her of being jealous.

"Well, it's all set, then. I'll give you the money for her passage and for the schooling."

"Betsy, have you decided? Are you coming?"

"There's no decision for me to make now, Edmund. If Mary goes, I can't. The money I give to her will be hers. She says she'll pay me back, but that could be years from now. There will be none for me to start over. Besides, I can hardly get lost in Boston and pretend to be a widow with a cousin alongside who knows the difference."

Her strong hands sliced off a wedge of dough, rolled and tucked, then squeezed it into a pan. She picked up a large, menacing-looking knife and sliced off another hunk of the dough and rolled it for the next loaf.

"I can pay your passage—"

"I don't take charity from nobody, understand that? We Elliotts don't take charity. No, Edmund, I won't be going to Boston. I'll stay here and take care of John. Mary gets the chance to go on and make a life for herself. I don't get to do that. And I can't take the boys away from their father. That'd be too selfish to talk about."

Edmund's disappointment was acute. While he was happy to do this good deed for Mary, he hadn't considered that it would prevent Betsy from going. It all made sense now. Damn, but he wanted Betsy to have a better life. He wanted her close to him, too. His feelings for her were beyond reason. It wasn't a good thing, to want a woman who was married, but it was what he felt. She was what he wanted.

"I love you, Betsy, you know that. I want you to come with me," he pleaded. "There's no life here for you, and the boys could go to a nice school in Boston. I know people who would buy your work, your sewing stuff, and you might be able to put it in shops. I could help you start a good life."

"I have a life. It's a hard one, and it's not a fancy Boston life, but it's mine. It all sounds good, what you say, but it's impossible. I got boys, I am married, I needs to stay. What would people think of me running off with you, anyway? I'd be shamed forever." She slammed another roll of dough into a pan.

"Who cares once you're gone? Boston is a big city, and nobody'd know you there, and you would have me to keep things good for you. I worry, you know. John's not right lately. You'll be all by yourself here in the house, with not even Mary, after I go."

A third thump echoed in the kitchen as the final ball of dough dropped into the last pan. The loaves were lined up along a shelf over the wood stove and covered with a long cloth, then a small baby quilt was placed over them to keep the dough warm while it rose. Baked bread was the biggest part of their diet, and as her family grew, so would this job. Mary's mother had ten youngsters and baked every single day. No wonder they were glad when Mary stayed with them—one less to feed.

The door opened with a gust, and Old Julie walked into the kitchen. Her keen eyes noted the seriousness on their faces. She picked up on their quick shift apart and the look of guilt and tucked the information into her mind to ponder later.

"Betsy, come with me. Mervina's boy is sick, and 'tis real bad. I think he has pneumonia. I don't know if he's going to make it. I've done what I can. I've put a fat pork poultice on, and I've given all I can in medicine. I can't get Dr. Malcolm over here, as he's off in Herring Neck to look after some folks over there that can't get to the Twillingate hospital. But he can't do no more than me, either. If that boy goes bad, she needs you, Betsy. God knows that man of hers is no good."

"Oh, God. Yes, I'll come. Edmund, tell John where I'm gone to."

Betsy made her way around the room, gathering a few items she might need, while Old Julie waited at the door. She wrapped herself in her warmest coat for the tickle where Mervina Bailey waited for some change in her son's condition.

* * * * *

"Oh, Mervina, how is he?" Betsy held her hand out to her friend.

"He's the same." She looked from Betsy to the midwife. "Julie, he is no better."

The little boy's grey face peeked over a mountain of quilts. The lack of oxygen was evident as his tiny body fought a losing battle. Julie rubbed his forehead and checked his lungs before giving a shake of her head.

"Is he gone?" Paddy Bailey wiped a hand through his ginger hair and closed his eyes. He didn't want the answer.

"Almost. I think you should sit by him."

"No, no, no, no! Not my boy!" Mervina wailed.

Her husband reached out and put his big arms around her, his body heaving with sobs. They made their way to the bed together. Mervina climbed in beside her son and pulled him into her arms. Her husband wrapped his arms around them both as their anguished cries filled the room.

Betsy stood back, allowing the parents to be with their son. Before long, poor Charlie slipped away as his heart stopped, his lungs swollen from the infection that had taken hold just two days before.

Old Julie cast her eyes to the ground, feeling helpless. People died too soon, and she often witnessed it. She was always called to nurse the worst of the sick and always showed up. There were times she saved a life, but most times in this place she watched life slip away. The hardest was losing youngsters who couldn't fight diseases the way the adults could.

Betsy bore witness to the loss, and her heart broke for the family. She mourned for young Charlie Bailey, who had been as good as her own. He had been over to her house so often, but now his smart mind and his sweet ways were gone forever. A light had been doused in all their lives.

There was a flicker as the kerosene lamp struggled for oxygen to feed its flame. The glow brightened again, illuminating a room of sorrow in a golden light.

Betsy struggled to keep her sadness inside. This was not her pain to bear, though it impacted her a great deal. How curious Charlie had been about airplanes and cod prices. He had played cat's cradle with Edmund and spoken like a much older child.

Mervina's mother was there, as were others from the community. The house slowly filled, and Betsy was able to remove herself from the room. Mervina's howls of pain were those of a wounded animal, spearing the night. A family member put a dram in some tea, and it sent her to sleep.

Her husband carried her to their room, his spirit defeated but his love for his wife obvious in his tender care of her during this time. Contrary to Old Julie's concern, Paddy Bailey was a big help. Gone was the blowhard braggart who had annoyed them all, to be replaced by a broken man with a love so deep for the mother of his child that he buried his own grief out of concern for hers. When some of the men came by to suggest they work on making the box, he asked that they do it for him. He had to tend to Mervina after this most tragic of losses.

Betsy noted his concern and wondered what it was like to have someone care for you that way. It felt like she was the one who did all the caring, with John being sick. What if it were her boys? What if it were she who had all she cared for stolen from her by some disease that came stalking through the community unannounced? Who would care for her? Who would console her? Certainly not John, who had a weak mind for such things. His distress was always the centre of their family life. She had no hope of ever leaving him, though, or of anyone caring that she stayed. Edmund might be like that. He seemed to want what was best for her over what was better for him. Surely, saddling himself with a married woman and two boys in Boston would be a burden for a single young bachelor, yet he had begged her to come.

Here, the most she could do was keep her own children alive as best she could. She couldn't fail at that, of all things.

Betsy felt selfish in her thoughts, for this was Mervina's loss. She finished up the dishes and informed one of Mervina's sisters that she would be leaving to go check on her own boys. She hugged her friend's aging mother and made her way toward the front door, pulling her coat tight. Her eyes adjusted to the dark as she started up the road toward her place. She had gone a short way, just twenty feet or so, when she heard a strange wailing sound. Startled, she stopped and listened, wondering if it were human. Sometimes a lynx at night sounded like a child screaming, but this was deeper.

"Paddy?"

Betsy knew it was him, though she hadn't seen him leave. She walked toward a large store he used as a workshop. There was no answer, but the wailing stopped, and she made her way to it, pulling the string that lifted the latch on the door. Paddy Bailey sat by the light of a small lantern, a dark form huddled with his face in his hands and his shoulders heaving as he tried to right himself.

"Go, Betsy, maid. I can't—it's best you go." He felt emasculated to be seen like this.

"Paddy, 'tis all right, 'tis all right. You're supposed to be sad. It's all right, it's only me." Betsy swept in and put her hand on the back of the man who was in so much pain.

"Oh, Betsy, what will I do? How will I live without my boy? How will Mervina go on? He was all she ever had! I know he's not mine. I know you heard the yarns on that around town, and I've always known that she got him by somebody else, but all she wanted was a youngster, and I don't care how he got to us. He was mine."

Betsy hadn't heard a single rumour about Mervina . . . but yes, it made sense. The boy didn't look like either of his parents, and it had taken so long for her to get pregnant.

"You don't know any of that, Paddy. Shut your foolishness, now. He was your boy. Everybody knew that. I never heard a sound otherwise, and sure, I would have heard, wouldn't I?"

"Yes, I suppose you would. Yes, he was my boy, my lovely boy, and he's gone." He sobbed again, and Betsy moved in and wrapped her arms around him. As he wept, she rocked him liked she rocked her own boys, and soon he drew one last, sorrowful sob inward before pulling himself together.

"I got to go back up for Mervina. Thank you, Betsy." Paddy's head was bowed. He was a man, and Betsy knew he was ashamed of his emotions.

"Now go on with you. Yes, you take care of Mervina, but watch yourself, too. You can't be no good for her if *you're* not good. If you needs to have a place to go sometimes, you come over and I'll make you a cup of tea and give you a bite of bread." *And a shoulder to lean on.*

"I might have to do that sometimes, Betsy, honest to God. I can't seem to talk to the men. They want to make stuff, fix a box for my boy. They're going to put my boy in a box. I can't do that. I knows I'm soft, that I'm to do that as a man, but I can't. I just want him back. I want Mervina to be happy again. I might need you to help me with that sometimes."

"I'm happy to help. Women thinks different on these things, so come over for a chat when you needs to. We got some hard days to get you and your wife through, now, and get through you will."

"I'm not sure we will, Betsy, but I'm going to try, for Mervina."

She nodded and took his elbow, and they walked back to the house with the lantern in hand. Betsy handed it to him a few feet from the house and watched him go around to the side door and enter without going through the kitchen. He wanted to avoid the crowd and be with his wife. That was how he had left without notice to grieve in private.

Betsy turned back and started her trek home, her steps slow and her mind full of sadness for the couple who now faced the world without their beautiful child. Amidst all her sorrow, between her thoughts of sadness, a piece of their conversation began to surface, and it would

not be tamped down by sorrow or the guilt of entertaining it at a time like this. For the entire walk and into the following days, there loomed a nagging question.

Now I wonder who had really owned Mervina's youngster, Betsy thought as she entered her home in the wee hours of the morning.

THIRTY-FIVE

Old Julie reached for another biscuit, her steady hand dropping nary a crumb as she pulled it to her plate. She looked around the large, tidy kitchen. The room sparkled from Betsy's care. Her own place was sparse and drafty, the walls grey where old wallpaper had faded and peeled, leaving sad, pale rosebuds visible in tired spaces where her late mother-in-law had tried to make a home.

She was grateful to have a place at all, she truly was. But sometimes she wondered what would have happened had John Elliott kept walking her home, if her late husband had not forced her into a horrible marriage, and if she hadn't shuttered herself away like a hermit so many years ago after his death, coming out only to help women give birth or prevent life from starting and to aid in some healing here and there. But it was no good to think of the past. Life was what it was—hard, cold, and if you were lucky, short.

Betsy bustled into the kitchen, straightening things up that weren't messy before pouring herself a cup of tea from the brown teapot and joining Julie at the table.

"We could have gone into the parlour. The fire is lit. Young Edmund started it for me before he took off. So, the boy is leaving, is he?"

"He says so," Betsy replied. "He heard that Earle is making a run for it tomorrow or the next day."

"Lewisporte, then St. John's for a steamer to Boston when it goes?"

"I s'pose. You heard young Mary is going with him?"

"Yeah, that's cute. I heard she's going to be a nurse."

"She has some ambitions. Wants to be a nurse and get married."

"Aw . . . the second is her bigger plan. Got a likin' for young Edmund, does she? Sure, she's pretty young for him."

"I'm pretty young for John."

"No lies. No lies at all, is it?" Julie laughed. Betsy had called her here for a reason. They were friends, but they didn't socialize like this.

"How's Mervina today?"

"Tore to pieces, like all the days. She's never going to get over it."

"I don't think I would. Did you ever lose one?"

"No. I'm lucky. I suppose the more you have the more likely you will."

"But poor Mervina, with only the one," Betsy said, blowing on her teacup.

"And it took so long to get that one," Julie replied, her eyes fixed on a place beyond Betsy's head.

"Who owned the boy, Julie?"

"What?" Julie shouldn't have been surprised at Betsy's straightforwardness, but she was nonetheless. Oh, they had all speculated on who that boy belonged to. Had anybody else asked, she'd have answered without thought as to who was the likely candidate.

"How was John when you looked in?" Betsy asked, realizing that should be her priority, not gossip.

"Same as last time. No change, Betsy. I don't know." Julie chewed a bit of the biscuit. It was lemony and crispy, and store-bought because there was money for that here at the Elliotts'. She shook her head at the thought of what John Elliott had become. He was awake, with a faraway look on his face and a smile. A strange smile. His heart and lungs were good, but he wasn't there in his mind.

"Okay, now tell me who owns the boy. Surely he wasn't Paddy's."

"No, he wasn't. I'll tell you, but you must promise not to tell a soul. I'll tell you as if you're a nurse or a midwife, and you have to keep it the same."

"She come to you? When she was expecting? Mervina did?"

"They all comes to me. But before that. She couldn't get with a baby. I mean, she was regular in her times and she had no reason to think it was her fault. Six years married. She said they was at it all the time, trying for a youngster. She wanted me to fix it, but I says, Mervina, 'tis likely Paddy. I can't tell him that, she says, he'll be savage. I needs a baby, how do I know it's him for sure? So, I says no way to find out except to try another fellow."

"That put the idea in her head?"

"I think the idea was already in her head, Betsy, but she wanted me to say it would work."

"And then she found a man?"

"Was not three months later she comes to me and says her time didn't come, so I checked her and said yes, I think Paddy finally done the job."

"And she told you it wasn't Paddy?"

"I didn't ask her. Not my place to do that. Since you're with me on the women and borning babies, you'll have to remember you needs to let them tell you stuff on their own and you can't repeat except to the other midwives."

"I understand. So, you're not going to tell me who the father might be?"

"I don't know for sure, but tell you what. You tell me what you really brought me here for, and I'll see."

"I brought you here to check on John and for tea."

"Don't lie, Betsy. You brought me here to tell me something you can't tell anybody else. Is it young Edmund? Are you and he having relations? Do you have something you wants me to take care of?"

"No, nothing like that. I don't have any problems I needs taking care of, but I do have something that just needs to be said to some-body."

"I'm as good as the dead for keeping stuff. I knows I just told you that about Mervina, but only because you is a midwife, too. We got to keep the women's stuff quiet together."

"Edmund asked me to move to Boston."

"So, there is something going on?" Julie knew it. She could see the way he looked at her.

"Nothing much, to be honest, but he says he loves me and wants me to go. I said no. There's no way for it, anyway. Mary is going, I got the boys, I got John, who needs caring for, and I'm married to him. I have to stay here, Julie, but I needed to say it to somebody."

"That you was invited to go?"

"That I'm *dying* to go. Some days I think if I stays here I'll die. Worse, that my boys will die. Boston has doctors. Edmund says that the young boy of Mervina's wouldn't have died in Boston, that they got medicine there for that pneumonia they don't have here. It has the best hospitals. Also, his crowd got money. Not so much as they once had because of the depression, but more than most. And he's coming into some of it. Not that I wants his money, because I got my own money, too. He said he can put me up, start me in a bit of a business, and get the boys in a good school. But I can't. I'm going to give the money I have to Mary because she's young and had such a hard time and needs to get out of this place. I said I would already.

"But oh, Julie, it should be me. I wants to be the young girl going off to find something in the world, to get off this godforsaken rock. Since I come here, I haven't even been so far as Fogo. Not that I wants to go to another place just like this one. Julie, don't you ever want to go to a big city and see what the world is like somewhere else?"

"I did one time, but not anymore. Now I just wants a quiet and peaceful life. But I understand, because one time I died to leave this place. My God, Betsy, go. Just go. If I had the chance you had at your age with me boys, I would have jumped on that boat without a thought."

"But you had a bad husband. I just have a sick one. I'm supposed to take care of him. He's in bed, and now I'm going to spend the rest of this winter taking care of him. Mary will be gone, Edmund will be gone, and I'll be doing it all myself. I can't stand it. But I got to do it. I signed up for it. Like those who signs up for war. They knows they could die in the mud, but they got to stay. I'm stuck in the mud, Julie."

"No, you're choosing to stay in the mud."

"I belongs in the mud. I signed up for the mud. I can't leave John, take his boys away."

"John keeps leaving you, don't he? Oh, I knows 'tis not his fault. But I remember how hard you had it when he was sick the last time.

He is in hard shape now. No guarantees there'll be any grub to eat in a month. I'm in people's houses, and I can tell you, these past years it's going down. Pure starvation is what it is. People going away in droves for work, no money for anything, and it's getting worse. No telling how bad off we'll be when we gets the rights of it all from this commission.

"I can't tell you to get out, and God knows I needs a hand, and you've been the one on my right these past years since you came here, but before you lets that boat leave without you, let me tell you something. I want you to make your choice, Betsy, knowing everything. I'm going to tell you something, and you got to think on it. Before you puts that girl on the boat instead of you, you need to know what you're doing."

"What? What is it I should know?"

"Well, first thing is this. When I checked on John, he didn't know those boys were in the world. Nor me or you. He might come out of it, he might not. I can't say he will, because he's worse than he's ever been. But he's not dying, Betsy. He might be like this for another forty years. He's a hearty man in body if not in mind. You stays and he don't get better, you're trapped with that."

"I know that."

"Well, here's the big news, and I want you to believe me. It's hard to say."

"Say it!" Betsy demanded.

"Mervina's boy was John Elliott's, Betsy. People seen her coming out of his old store loft when you had your first one. The timing is right. She wanted a baby for herself, and she got one out of John Elliott."

"That's a lie!" Betsy stood, her eyes widening, her protective instinct for her husband rising to the surface.

"No, it's no lie. I am not a liar, and you knows it. Think about it. Think hard about it, Betsy. That boy was the spittin' image of your boys except for the lighter hair. That's because George and Richard got yours. But the way they talk, the way he talked, the shape of his face. That's all John Elliott. You needed to know that. Decide how much you really owe John Elliott, since he didn't even owe you a bit of respect when he was going at Mervina Bailey while you were laid up after having his son."

Betsy's entire body shook with despair, rage, denial, and finally, hatred. She had not taken John for that kind of man. He was always at her, for she never denied him that except when she couldn't. But John never said no to nobody in his life. If Mervina wanted him, he'd go for her. The truth struck her like a rock in the side of the head.

"I can't think on this right now. I can't even go into the room to check on John. I might stick a knife right through his gut if the mood strikes me. You're going to have to stay with me until Edmund gets home, because I might go in an' kill the man stone dead."

"You won't, Betsy, but now you know. If you go, know this, too. I'll see that John is tended to. I got nothing at my place. 'Tis hardly fit to live in. I'll come here to watch over him if you go. Make sure he's alive and fed. I takes care of people all the time, and one more is no hardship for me. I get a bit for my work, free wood and grub enough to feed us. Take the boys, get out of this place, go find the world. Go find Boston."

Betsy stood awhile, and Julie watched her. She stared out the window toward the west, where the run had opened. The boat would make it through to Lewisporte, and from there a train to St. John's. Her path was before her. She couldn't go with Edmund, could she? Could she walk away from it all? Take her sons and go? Or should she stay and do what she was supposed to do? She hated the word *supposed*. It was a vile word that kept her tied down and strung up all at once. She knew what she was *supposed* to do. That had been hammered into her brain from the moment of birth. Girls got married and took care of everybody else.

Now, if she could only figure out what she was *going* to do.

THIRTY-SIX

Edmund found Betsy sitting at the table later that night. It was the first time he'd ever seen her still, her near-constant movement at rest. She gave no notice to his entry into the house.

"Are you all right, Betsy? Where are the boys?"

"The boys are with Old Julie, and I'm fine," she snapped, not moving her eyes from a spot ahead of her on the table.

"Is it because we're going tomorrow? Is that what's wrong?"

Edmund ignored her curt attitude. It was a cover for her troubles. The more disturbed she was, the angrier she got. Combined with this stillness of hers, it was even worse. He knew she was worried. He was worried, too. Leaving her with an ill husband and two children after her friend Mervina's tragedy concerned him. Edmund didn't want to leave, but he couldn't make her go. He had given up trying to convince her. The best thing for him to do was reassure her that she would be fine, though he wasn't even sure that she would be.

"Look, Betsy. I still want you to come, but I understand why you can't. I really do. I'm going to go to Earle's tonight because he wants me to help load up a horse Jacob Edwards sold to a man in Laurenceton, and I'm good with the horses. Jacob's got that bad leg, or he'd do it himself. The boat is leaving at nine. You'll bring Mary to the boat? I hear she wants to spend tonight with her mother and father and family before coming to you in the morning to say goodbye. Is that the luggage?" Edmund nodded at an old suitcase and a trunk by the door. Next to it was a large sack-like bag.

Betsy nodded and lifted herself up.

"I'll take them with me tonight," Edmund said.

"Yes. Take them with you tonight."

He swept around the table and put his arms out to her, braver than he'd ever been, his desire to comfort her somehow, to have her near one more time, stronger than his fear of her sharp words. She reached out and held his hand in hers for a moment. She met his eyes. With lips pursed and cheeks damp, her red-rimmed eyes sought comfort. She moved closer to him, and he pulled her in, holding her in his arms as she sobbed. He let her cry. Betsy loved him. Edmund was certain of it. He knew he loved her. But she was duty-bound to stay, and he was hell-bent to leave. He kissed her hair, and she moved away.

"I should feed you before you take off. I'll pack you a lunch to take tonight, too. Can you bring along a lunch?"

"Yes, I can bring along whatever you make. I have the horse and carriage from Jacob to bring my stuff. I'm going to load it up now, and then I'll come have a bit of tea."

"Say goodbye to John," Betsy said.

"Will he know?"

"He might. I tell him all the news, and sometimes he understands. I told him about young Charles Bailey. I'm sure he understood that. It's better you did than you didn't, just in case."

"Yes, of course I will."

Edmund brought his belongings to the door and set them beside the suitcase, eyeing Betsy as she packed up bread, cake, and biscuits—enough for a month, he figured. There was food to buy along the way, but her baking was hard to turn down. Mary would enjoy some treats, too, he thought. While the girl was excited to go, he knew she would feel a bit homesick. A few of Betsy's buns might make her day.

John sat in bed, propped up against pillows, his eyes closed. Edmund walked to him and reached out, touching his arm. John looked far younger than he had before, his face smooth from bedrest and the lack of hardship on his mind.

"Thank you for everything, John. You were awful kind, and you know that my book will have your name in the acknowledgements. I will be sure to send you copies for yourself and Betsy. When you feel better, you'll want to read it all. I'm going back to start in practice, once I pass the exam. I'm taking young Mary with me. She's going to nursing school, but she'll do some service work for the family until then. Thank you for lending her the money for it. It's a kindness she'll never forget."

John smiled and opened his eyes.

"Mere was nice to you, was she? She is nice to me. I thinks it's good that you're going back to the college."

Edmund started. It was the first time John had spoken since the death of the young Bailey boy.

"You're all right, John?"

"I'm the best kind, b'y," John agreed. "Got me Mere with me, me youngsters. I just needs a nap. Have a good trip and send me those books from the Boston college. I likes to have me name in a book. Is you putting any other men's names in it?"

"Not from here, no. Just yours."

"Can you put one in for me? Because he might need his name in a book more than I do."

"Yes, of course. Who is that?" Edmund could no more deny John Elliott than he could fly.

"Put young Bailey's name in the book—Paddy. I think he needs a bit of a boost, and he'd like that. Just a thank you for his help would be a good thing, don't you think? He might not be the best kind of man, but he's a better man than me in a lot of ways that you don't need to know about. Can you put his name in the book? Take mine out, p'raps, and put his in?"

"I will do that, rest assured, John. I'll put both in, and yes, that's a thoughtful kindness, for sure. After his loss, he may need a nice hand up. And I'll make sure a copy goes to him, too."

"That's fine. Now Mere is coming, so I got to go. I hope I can stay this time. Goodbye, Edmund."

"Goodbye, John."

John continued to stare across the room, a slight smile on his lips. Edmund waved his hand in front of him, and he didn't blink. Whatever happened to John in these fits made him content, if unreachable.

Edmund left the room, troubled by a man who seemed to live with a foot in two worlds. He wondered when he would step fully into the other world, because he suspected that John's gentle mind was all but done with this one.

In the kitchen, Betsy handed him a large box full of food.

"Thank you, Betsy. It's far too much, but I'm sure we'll eat all of it."

"It's just the right amount, don't worry. How was John?"

"He spoke to me, Betsy." He didn't tell her John had mentioned Mere. It might bother her that he was thinking of his first wife.

"What?"

Dear Lord, was he coming to? God help her, what if he was? Betsy didn't know what would be harder to cope with, John waking up or John sleeping forever. Living with the revelation from Julie had taken the strength from her. She felt herself wanting to cry, to throw herself into Edmund's arms again and tell him all that she knew, to relieve herself of the burden of it all. Instead, she straightened herself up and walked to the door.

"Well, 'tis time for you to go. Get on, you better get out. I'll hang on and close the door for you."

"Okay, Betsy. Thank you, and goodbye," Edmund said, coming back inside one last time when everything was out of the house.

She turned toward the kitchen and stared, and he left a moment later, heart heavy. Betsy watched him hop on the back of the sleigh and snap the reins. He glanced back once, and she looked away.

The small pony shook its head once, bells jingling, then moved forward with a jolt before speeding up to a trot.

THIRTY-SEVEN

The next morning, Mary entered the warm kitchen and stomped the snow off her boots.

"Betsy, Edmund, I'm here! I'm ready to go. Mom and Dad says they'll meet us at the wharf just before we leave."

She was wearing her best dress. She owned just two, but she hoped that the money Betsy was giving her would be enough to buy at least one more when she got to Boston. Or to buy material to make one.

Old Julie walked in. "Hello, Mary, my dear. Have a seat."

"Oh!" the girl said, surprised. "Yes, sure. I just thought I'd come a bit early, you know, and not keep anybody waiting. Is Edmund here? I didn't see the horse."

"Let me get you some tea. Edmund is already gone. He went to his uncle's for the night. Said he had to help Earle's man, so he wouldn't be back before the trip."

"Oh, Okay. Do I have time for tea?"

"Yes, and I think you need a drop," Julie said, not relishing the task before her. She had brought young George and Richard home late and stayed the night, checking on John before she retired.

"Where is Betsy? Where are the boys? I needs to say goodbye to 'em. Is me and Betsy walking to the wharf? I only got this little bag. I can carry it if the horse is gone."

"Mary, sit down. Here, have the tea."

"Is something wrong, Mrs. Julie?" Mary had been startled to find her and not Betsy in the kitchen, but then, with Mr. Elliott so sick, it was not so surprising.

"Betsy is gone, my love. She took the boys, and she is gone to Boston with Edmund. I'm moving up here to take care of John."

"What? Betsy is going, too? She can't! She's married. She has to stay with her husband. I should go catch the boat. I better leave. She told me it was leaving at eleven. I have to catch up with her and Edmund!"

"The boat is gone, Mary. The boat left nine o'clock. I saw her go across the run. She's an hour gone now, I allow."

"What? How will I get there?"

"You're not going, Mary. Not this time. Betsy decided to go instead. She left me this note for you. Now sit down and read it."

Mary sat, her face a portrait of distress and confusion. She was to go to nursing school if Edmund didn't propose to her first. She had her plans. Betsy wasn't going. What was this about? With shaking hands, she opened the note that was left for her. It was short and blunt and honest.

> *Dear Mary,*
>
> *I have decided that I am going to Boston with Edmund. John is sick and cannot care for us. Edmund can help me take care of the boys. I am sorry, but I'm sure your time to leave will come in another way. But it won't be to Boston,*

and not with Edmund. Not this time. I am sorry for the dis-
appointment you feel right now, but you will find your own
way. Today, I'm finding mine.

    Betsy

Mary's hand trembled as she looked at Julie, acceptance hard to
come by. This betrayal was worse, in some ways, than being violated
in the back room of this house. With a loud wail, she jumped up from
the table and ran out of the house, leaving the door swinging on its
hinges.

Julie's heart was heavy for the child. She closed the door and
turned back to the kitchen where she now lived with John Elliott. The
pretty wallpaper, the view of the cove out the back window, the man
who lay ill in his mind in the room beyond, all gave her a sense of
peace that even the dramatic departure of the heartbroken young girl
couldn't dampen. Caring for people was what Julie had always done,
and tending to John Elliott would be no burden for her. She had no
ambitions beyond continuing her work, and now she could do it from
the luxury of the Elliott house. What had been a burden to a young
Betsy, who was full of dreams and ambition, was a pleasure to one
whose life was as hard as Julie's. This was the best Julie had had it in
her life, and she was bound and determined to keep it that way.

* * * * *

Edmund soothed the black mare as the boat headed through Dil-
do Run. He gave her nose one last rub when she was calm and made
his way to the wheelhouse. The captain eyed the horizon.

"It's pretty open for April, but there is some ice coming in far off. Wind has been off the land for a long time. We might have an early spring. Keep your eyes open for a seal, if you can. We see one, we got the gun ready for it. Might take a bit of a traipse across the ice, but a nice swile would be a good feed for the run back tomorrow."

"Many passengers below?" Edmund asked.

"Just the three. More freight than fares," the skipper said. "The young lady said she was with you? She was here very early, before me, waiting when I got here. They all were. The others were already down below. You were still off getting the horse, and Frank and Jimmer weren't here yet." He referred to his crewmen, who were busy working on deck.

"She must have been excited to come so early." Edmund was surprised Mary wasn't all over him on the deck, but perhaps she was a bit nervous to be leaving. Or maybe seasick.

"I can't say. Never had a chance to talk much to her."

It disappointed him that he wouldn't get to see Betsy once more. Their parting was cold. There were things to say, but he ended up too busy with the horse to go back up for one final goodbye. He hadn't had time to make sure Mary had made it aboard, either, but he knew Betsy would follow through with whatever needed to be done.

He thought ahead to the next few months. They would take the train to St. John's to finish up his business there and to hand in the book he'd written to a publisher. Now that his dissertation was finished, it wouldn't be long before his trust fund was released. It was a condition of the bequeathal. While it was smaller than it would have been before the crash, his late uncle had been smart and distrusted the stock market, saving them all from becoming destitute.

They would take passage on the first boat heading to Boston. They could beat the ice if they could get on a ship soon enough. Navigation was rough in the spring, but it was still possible. He had secured accommodations for him and Mary in his friend Michael's house until then. Michael had gone away to Toronto for work. Edmund guessed he needed the bit of board money, given how fast his friend had accepted his offer. These times were hard. He was hearing things were rough in Boston, too, but a job awaited. Mr. Felene had helped him land it, and it would do until he was licensed to practise.

Edmund made his way down the steps into the galley where passengers sat during a crossing. He noted still shapes under the blankets in the bunks normally reserved for the captain and crew. They only needed the blankets at night while the boat was docked away from home. During passage, travellers often napped in them to avoid seasickness.

Edmund walked toward Mary, wondering where the other two passengers were. She was alone at the table in the middle of the tiny room. A wood stove gave the compartment enough warmth, but she still wore a fur coat. He recognized it. Betsy must have given it to her, he thought, before realization struck.

"Betsy?" he whispered, his heart leaping.

"Yes," she said strongly, lifting her head.

"You're here? Where is Mary?"

"Is it okay that I'm here?"

"It is where you should be, but I didn't think you would ever. . . . When did you decide to come?"

"I knew when I saw you last night, but I couldn't say the words. So many things need to be said. Just listen."

"The boys? How?" Edmund glanced at the bunks.

"Yes, tucked in sound. I was up all night, woke them up real early, walked us over around the back point, and snuck aboard before light. 'Twas my bags you brought with you, not Mary's. Julie gave me something to help them sleep, and they have been out for a while. First they were excited, of course, but I wanted to be sure they didn't get seasick. You know that young captain? That was a bit of luck. I never met him before, so I told him my name was Mary. Told him two more were in the cabin, and he was so busy, his first trip for Mr. Earle and all, so I gave him the fare for all of us, and he never even come down here. I'm glad, because nobody needs to know I'm gone right away.

"Now, let me tell you what I need to before they wake up. Because I just done a very wrong thing, and though it was your idea, Edmund, I knows you'll think less of me someday for it. Everybody will, but I didn't leave just on a—what's the right word?"

"Whim?"

"Yes, that's a good one, and no, it wasn't."

"Tell me, Betsy. We've a few hours yet to the dock. Why did you decide to leave?"

THIRTY-EIGHT

"It goes back a long time, Edmund. To my father. Do you know that when a person dies of fever there is a smell to it? It was like that when Father died. The walls and beams of the house stank. It was a combination of sour breath, sweaty sheets, and—God, Edmund—hopelessness. I remember it like it was yesterday. But shabby as it was, it was my home. I even thought that the paint on the faded, grey boards with small, grey hairs of wood that stuck out through the blue was pretty. Oh, it wasn't Elliott pretty, but it was pretty to me."

"It sounds like a lovely place."

"No, it was awful. But it was home. It was hot that day. Right sultry. The air stuck your clothes to your skin like a wet wool garnsey. It was August month. He looked so bad."

Betsy recalled her father's blue eyes peering from craters on either side of a nose that was crimson in a grey-skinned face. He was covered by a quilt whose faded patches had specks of blue calico that matched his eyes. As hot as it was, he had stopped sweating. There was nothing left in him to come out.

"I had to help care for him. I was the oldest. He said stuff to me that I never forgot."

"Tell me what he said, Betsy," Edmund prodded, his eyes fast on her face, hands clasped on the table before him.

Betsy's words transported her and Edmund to the room where a young girl had heard the final words of a beloved parent.

* * * * *

"If I don't make it, Betsy girl, remember, I done my best to make sure you had a good life."

"You did that, Father. I love your yarns."

"I know, but the stories weren't the point."

"What was the point, Father?"

"The point was that there is more in this world than you see. I grew up in a small bay, and I never left it until the war. Then I spent time in Africa, and I saw things me mind had no idea was there, and it made me different."

"Different how?"

"It changed me to know there was stuff out there. It give me a choice. When the war ended, I could have stayed and been an officer, but I come back here because this is where I love to be. This is where my family was. This is the path I took, Betsy, but I chose it fair and square, and I wouldn't have walked anywhere different."

"I'm happy that you came back, Father."

"I'm happy, too, and I never looked back once and said I should have gone a different way. And that's what I mean, my love. My stories weren't about leaving or staying, or one being better than the other is. It's about the road you take, Betsy, the choices you make."

"I'll do my best to do things that Mother tells me and be good."

"It's good to be good, but don't do it because your mother says so, Betsy. Do it because your heart tells you to. Your life is yours. I come home and I took exactly the path I wanted to. Oh, they say I was a bit touched, I s'pose, but I was always happy. I am happy to go, because I chose my life. You will have choices, too, my dear, and I want you to do the same."

"Okay, Father, I will."

* * * * *

A lump formed in Betsy's throat after she finished telling Edmund the last talk she had with her father. She could bake bread and knit a sweater, but her lessons in life still hadn't extended to the ability to cope with the profound grief her father's passing had left her.

"But there was no choice for me, Edmund. They shipped the youngsters off on the steamer to the orphanage, and me and Mother travelled off to the Elliotts."

Edmund let out a breath. He, too, had lost his father, and he knew that heartache well.

"I remember taking the steps to that house, knowing life was over for me as much as it was for my father. I'd seen how my mother lived, sad and angry at a life of drudgery. Then she died one day while making the bed in the old lady's room. Everybody thought me and John should get married, and I couldn't see any other good option. Know what? I was happy about it. I thought I'd be safe. Yes, he's a lot older, but he's a good man, if farther from perfect than I once thought."

"He is sick, too."

"He is that, Edmund. And I didn't know he was sick as he is.

The first winter was hard, but he got better, and I thought it was just the grippe. They never told me that he had such a bad sickness. Oh, I should have known, but the mind is a queer thing. I could talk myself out of his being so bad as he was, because I wanted him to be. I thought it might be easier than marrying some of the others who came around who never had a nice house and their own schooner, and I thought a wife had a better chance than a serving girl.

"Oh, I know, Edmund, that it won't be easy with two youngsters in a strange place, and I also know I can't ever go back now, because I'm ruined. But I realized that Father told me that this is my choice, this life is my path to walk, so I decided I'm going to do some of that walking in Boston."

Edmund took Betsy's hand.

"I feel bad about Mary, though," she said.

"We can figure out something for Mary. She's young. She'll have other chances."

"So, that's it, then. We're going to Boston?"

Edmund caught a glimpse of a young girl underneath all the hardness that made up the woman he loved. He grasped her other hand, and they held on to each other across the table.

"Yes. You, Betsy Elliott, are going to Boston."

The boat continued to punch forward, knocking aside the odd pan of ice. The rocking motion helped keep the boys asleep in their bunk. The sun broke out above deck, and brilliant shards of light darted through a small window, painting Betsy and Edmund's hands with golden streaks. Out the little porthole, the ice frozen along the railings dripped as the day warmed and a light southwesterly wind puffed across the bay.

The vessel tugged on through, and when she was near the edge of the treacherous run before entering the Bay of Exploits, a sudden wave of fear washed over Betsy. She really could never go back. Nobody knew what had happened to Clyde Waugh, that was a secret, but this shame, it was public, and the people back home would never welcome her again. John, the man who had betrayed her, had also saved her at one point. Was she just shrugging off the weight of one hard life for the difficulties of another? She hardly knew what she was doing, only that she was going to be a Boston girl. What did that even mean? Had she made a huge mistake?

She glanced at the boys sleeping in the bunk and looked at Edmund, whose eyes were alight with some sort of foolish glint. She was free, and there were hospitals if the boys got sick, but she read the news. She was headed to a place with long unemployment lines, where the depression, as they called it, required some people to line up for hours for a bit of food. What if she ended up homeless,? What of the boys? Had she doomed them to poverty? At least on the island they had a roof over her heads and food in their little bellies.

Edmund was the key. She'd better keep on his good side until she figured things out or she'd wind up on the Boston dole. She coaxed a smile across her face, and Edmund returned it.

"What are you thinking now?" he asked.

"I'm thinking that my father said all that stuff, and now that I've finally done what I needed to do, I feel like I don't want to walk in Boston anymore." She smiled more as his face fell. Yes, he was the way to her success. Everything she said or did affected him. That was good.

"You don't?"

"No, Edmund, I don't. It's too slow. Walking, I mean. It's something I did to get from the house to the well and back. It's what I did when I went from bread baking to nursing John to feeding youngsters. When I get to Boston, once I stretch my legs a bit, I want to run! You'll help me, won't you? Run a ways with me?" She looked up at him.

Relief crossed over his face. His laughter echoed through the small cabin, and Betsy raised her fingers to her lips with another quick glance to the bunks.

"You can run as far and as fast as you want, Betsy, my love. I'll be there to take care of you. You know I'll keep you safe."

Betsy nodded, satisfied.

They sat, hands clasped, each thinking of the future. He saw a life with Betsy, helping her raise her two boys, and perhaps one day she would be free. Until then, he'd do all he could to help her out and keep her happy. Betsy's thoughts, however, lurked longer in the crevasse between the life she had left behind and the one to which she travelled. She would miss it all, as hard as it was.

Eventually, she breathed in and brought herself to where she was right now. On a boat, going away. She would find out soon enough if she' had made the right choice. Betsy squeezed Edmund's hand tighter, as though to make sure he was still there. Until then, she would focus on what was right in front of her, as she always had, and what was before her was Edmund Taylor.

At least for now.

ACKNOWLEDGEMENTS

For such a solitary endeavour, the writing of a book sure does require help from a lot of people. I am exceedingly grateful to all who have in some way contributed to this work. Thank you Crystal Gale-Brace for wading through early drafts. My immense gratitude to the amazing Donna Morrissey, editor extraordinaire, for being honest and brilliant in your feedback and for suggesting the title that ended all my angst. Special thank you to Ian Foster, whose song "The Calendar" provided the theme music as I pounded the keys in the early draft of this work. I also am thankful for authors who have inspired me on this journey, particularly Lia Mack, Kate Sparkes, Candace Osmond, Bill Rowe, Gary Collins, and Joel Thomas Hynes. From each of you I've gained valuable wisdom that keeps me moving forward in this crazy racket. Special thanks to the Cranfords, Garry, Margo, and Jerry, as well as the rest of the Flanker Press team. Your friendship, professionalism, and support, as well as your humour, made this journey a true pleasure. You're the best. And finally, and most of all, to Kent, Alyssa, Christina, Sophia, and Martina, thank you for your unwavering support. You are the inspiration.

Carolyn R. Parsons is a proud fisherman's daughter born and raised on Change Islands, Newfoundland and Labrador. She spent twenty-five years in Ontario, returned home to Newfoundland in 2012, and now resides in Lewisporte. An advocate for social issues, she was co-chair and spokesperson for the *Manolis L* Citizens Response Committee, which lobbied government to remove oil that threatened the marine environment from the sunken cargo ship in Notre Dame Bay.

She penned a regular community column entitled "Connections," a biweekly arts feature, "In Conversation," and wrote general news for the *Pilot*. Today she writes a weekly column, "Art & Soul," for the *Central Voice* and co-hosts an online radio program, *Bridges*. A founding director of Literary Events NL, she also serves as the current Central/Burin representative for the Writers' Alliance of Newfoundland and Labrador (WANL).

Carolyn is married to Kent Chaffey, also a Change Islander, and they have four daughters and three grandchildren. In the past decade, she has written a poetry collection, two novels, and a book of short stories. *The Forbidden Dreams of Betsy Elliott* is her debut novel with Flanker Press.